MW00605397

ALWAYS
Forward

By:

CECILIA GARCIA

Copyright

Copyright 2021 Cecilia A. Garcia

All rights reserved. No part of this book may be reproduced or used in any manner without the prior written permission of the copyright owner, except for the use of brief questions or passages in a book review.

Always Forward is a military fiction novella. All characters and events in this book are fictitious. Locations and descriptions of events may be similar to real historical events, and any similarities to actual persons, living or dead, are coincidental and not intended by the author.

Credits of cover design and images to Audrie Phoenixa and Ji Chen.

Printed in the United States of America.

Content Warning

Always Forward is a fictional novella with graphic content which depicts scenes of combat, post-traumatic stress flashbacks, and sexual trauma. There are also graphic descriptions of injuries that may be difficult for some readers. If you or someone you know is dealing with a type of trauma or this book uncovers the trauma you, the reader, need to deal with, know that you are not alone. Please reach out to the Mental Health America crisis line at 1-800-273-TALK (8255) or text MHA to 741741 at the Crisis Text Line.

Acknowledgments

This story has lived in my head for close to seventeen years, which means there have been so many individuals throughout the years that have been there for me and supported me along the way. It's so odd to start this way, but in some ways, I need to thank my good old Uncle Sam for deploying me to Iraq in 2004. Even though it was hell, Emily's story never would have come to me if I hadn't gone through my combat tour.

To my battle buddy, Shane, we may have bickered and fought a ton on our missions across the deserts of Iraq and the streets of Baghdad, but you helped me build the baseline for Emily's story. I will never forget our storytelling sessions in Lurch (our nickname for our truck), and I am so grateful you made it out of there alive, even if you left an eye behind. Thank you for always supporting me and being the best little brother/friend I could ask for.

To my two dearest girlfriends, Kate and Veronica, you both are the most supportive and positive friends I could ever ask for. I know it's not easy to be friends with a person who lives with PTSD, but you both never gave up on me, and I do not know where I would be without either of you in my life.

My mentor, a long-time friend, and overall queen of an author, A. A. Lewis. I literally would not be here if it weren't for your push to get this story out of my head. You have helped me along the entire journey, and I am entirely grateful for all your support, guidance, and motivational speeches. You are the iconic vision of what women helping women is all about. Thank you!

A big thank you to my beta readers, who were all strangers to me before this journey began; Ricci, Stephanie, Jamie, Thomas, and Armando. Your feedback and input on the book helped me grow as a writer so much. To Stephanie, my self-proclaimed hype-woman, thank you for believing in Always Forward!

My mother- Carolyn and my late father- Nick, you raised me to never give up and to always be the hardest working person in the room. Thank you for believing in me enough to sign over your custodial rights to the US Army of your seventeen-year-old daughter. I am the woman I am today because of you both. I wish dad could be here to read this, but I know he is with me in spirit.

To my daughters, Alesandra and Annalecia, you two are my everything. I love you with my entire being, and everything I have done and continue to do is for the two of you. You both are extremely brave, strong, and intelligent women, and if you learn anything from this book and the journey it took to write it, you can do anything you want in this world. It might take a decade to get it right, it might mean there will be heartaches and failures, but you can do whatever it is that makes your heart happy.

And last, but never least, to my husband, Milo. I don't think there are enough words in the English language for me to express the love and gratitude I have for you. You have been by my side for the past twenty-one years, and you never bat an eye at any of my crazy and wild ideas. You are my rock and my yin to my yang. You keep me solid and steady when I bring chaos to our lives. Thank you doesn't seem like enough, but it's a good thing I have a few more books on writing to express my undulated love for you.

TABLE OF CONTENTS

Prologue

EMILY

~

Milk. All I want is milk. Fresh cold milk. It's funny how that's what I think about. I can't remember the last time I had anything to drink. I try to keep track of the days and nights in here. It's hard. I only see daylight through a small crack in the hatch. I have no idea where I am or who else is here with me. I heard voices for a while, but not for what has to be at least a day or two.

All I know is I am in a hole in the ground with a hole to pee and shit in. I still can't remember what happened.

The burns on my legs are beginning to stink. Maggots are in the wound on my left leg. I picked out the shrapnel, but I have nothing to keep the maggots out. I guess they are the closest thing I have to antibiotics. The blood on my head finally slowed down and has stopped dripping to my eyes. I don't dare touch my forehead because I fear how bad the wound may be. I know head injuries tend to bleed more, but this feels worse than just a flesh wound.

I go through the list of names of the guys in my truck; Rodriguez, Simmons, and Grant. I call out for them again. "Rodriguez, Simmons, Grant!" This becomes the chant I repeatedly repeat until I am so tired and thirsty that I shut my eyes again and try not to pass out.

'God, a glass of milk is all I want right now,' I silently thought.

Chapter One

EMILY

Sometimes, I have moments of clarity, little flashbacks of a different time. A time when I had a purpose. A time when I was a leader, someone that was looked up to. I was a mom and a soldier. I was a wife, sister, daughter, and best friend. I served a purpose. Some could say that I gave up and stopped fighting for a way out. It's easy to say these things, I'm sure. Who knows, maybe people think I am dead.

I genuinely have no idea. I have been isolated from the world for so long. My only purpose now is to birth child after child. I am a breeding ground for the next generation. I pray this next generation will not be this evil as the current one. I try with all my heart to love these children, but I don't honestly see them as my own. My children had green eyes and ashy blonde hair. My children were brought into this world out of love between a man and woman, who committed their lives together. These children, all eight (8) of them, were born from rape and hatred. The truth is that it's not their fault. They didn't ask for this, more so than I did.

The moment of clarity that comes to me today is right after my youngest 'real' daughter was born. I remember holding her and her big sister, singing a lullaby to her. I strain to remember the words, but those have faded. I remember the look of pure unadulterated love on my oldest daughter's face, and then, the moment is gone; a mist floating back out the way it came in.

I hear the door to our hut slam shut. He is back; he always comes back. He hasn't laid a hand on me in quite some time, but I still shuffle to the corner of the hut. Then again, I haven't given him a reason to hurt me. I stopped trying to run away three births ago. I haven't seen anyone from the US military in years. I gave up getting out and succumbed to the notion that I will die here. At some point, I will not be able to breed any longer, and then I will be executed. I can only hope for an easy and clean death. I cower in the corner until he passes by me. Once he goes into the next room, I hurry outside.

The sunlight is piercing my eyes. After all these years, I still have not become accustomed to the heat and how bright the sun can be in the mid-afternoon.

"Abia, Lulu, Khayru. Come, now!" I call my younger three back to the hut. They have been playing stickball with the other kids in the village that are their age. It is time for them to help prepare dinner. Since their father is home, I must prepare a traditional dinner.

Asad, the baby, still clings to me in his wrap. I pray he is the last one I am forced to breed. The last few have been complicated pregnancies; I'm not sure I can do this again. He tells me all the time that 'I am so lucky' and how I should 'thank him' for saving me. This is not being saved. This is hell, but I press on. The three younger ones run to me and know without me saying a word what time it is. Abia and Lulu grab the pails to retrieve water from the village well. Khayru comes with me, and even though he is only three, he is as helpful as he can be. He comes to the back of the hut with me to entertain his baby brother, Asad, while I begin preparing dinner. The oldest four are at school. I had to beg Mohammed, their father, to allow the girls to attend. I only know English, having picked up the very basics of Arabic. Their father had to teach them to speak fluently in Arabic, whereas I secretly taught them English. I did my best to teach them proper English with the hopes that if one day they get out of this hell hole, they have an advantage in the real world.

Most of them look like their father, which is terrifying to me. It saddens me to see his face in so many innocent children. The youngest three, though, are different; they have my eyes. I have no idea how that could be, but they do. Those jade green eyes that I would see staring right back at me when I used to be able to look into a mirror. The same color eyes as my true daughters. The youngest is even showing signs of having blonde hair. I'm not sure how well that will fair him growing up, but it is the cards he has to deal with.

Abia and Lulu return with the water, and we get to making dinner. I have been roasting lamb all day and begin to boil water for the rice. Right now, we are fortunate enough to have been able to grow a small garden before the dry heat truly hits our region. I chop up veggies for the rice and have the younger children set the place inside to eat. When Mohammed is not around, the children and I are allowed to eat rice alone. He only provides a runner with meat the day before returning from one of his trips. I am not allowed to go to the market or enter the center of the village. I am confined to our hut and directly outside. I have 'earned' this right, as he says over the last few years.

In the earlier years, I ran every chance I could get. I had no idea where I would go or what I could do, but I had to try. I would fight back, scratch, and claw my way out. When I couldn't walk, I would crawl and dig into the hardened earth with my hands, fighting with every movement to escape. Each time a man, one of his guards would bring me back, dragging me through the streets. All of the villagers knew who I was, but they could do nothing to help me. If they tried to help me, they would be signing their death sentence.

The older kids return home from school and immediately begin their chores around the hut; picking vegetables, taking care of the garbage, and ensuring the younger ones are not making a mess.

He hates messes. Though he has never laid a hand on any of the children, the older ones have witnessed what he is capable of with me. They do not understand where I came from or who I truly am, but they know that I am their mother. Their urge to protect me is the only thing I can say I am grateful for here.

I begin to shave the meat away from the skewer it is on. I am careful not to let any meat fall to the ground. There are severe consequences for wasting food. Now, I am finally allowed to eat more than once a day. For years, I lived off the scraps from his plate and eventually from the children. After Asad was born, he said I 'earned the right' to more than one meal a day. As I cut the meat away from the skewer, I looked at the knife in my hands and thought back to the last time I tried to stab the monster. That earned me a month in a hole in the ground. No food but only enough water once a day to keep me from reaching complete dehydration. I was three months pregnant with what would have been Lulu's younger sibling, but I miscarried in that hole. I bled out in that god-forsaken hole in the ground, which was my hell. I stare at the knife again now, but I consider my choices with a clearer mind this time. If I was to use the knife on anyone, it might as well be on me.

I tell all the children to wash up. We don't have any form of running water in our village, just the communal well. But we are lucky that the well is not that far from our hut. The children have water more accessible than many families. I am not allowed to bathe entirely. I am lucky if I am allotted a damp rag to wipe the dirt from my hands and face. Since I am not allowed to leave the hut, I can only rely on what water is leftover after the children are clean and have enough to drink. There is no chance in this world that he would allow me to go with the children to the well. Trust me, after trying to escape so many times earlier on, he always has someone watching me, even when I can't see them. As I wipe away the day's dirt from my hands, I pull up my sleeves and see the faded tattoo in cursive on my wrist. The words are so faded that they are not even legible anymore, but I know what it says. This has been my only physical reminder of another lifetime. I try not to look at it often since the meaning behind it saddens me. The old Emily would have never given up or been broken, yet here I am, broken down and waiting for my execution.

I hear him coming up to the back steps of the hut. I quickly finish cleaning up and go outside to finish preparing the meal. The older children help me bring in the platters as he is waiting to eat. He has invited one of the elders to join us for dinner. This means that the female children and I will not be allowed to eat inside. The girls and I serve the men and then wait outside until my oldest, Mahir, signals that we can come in and make our plates. I keep my head down as I prepare the little ones' plates and then my own. We move back outside as quickly and quietly as possible. The two men are talking in hushed tones with Mahir. I cannot understand them since my Arabic is so broken up, but I know it is serious, judging from the looks on their faces.

After dinner, he takes the elder back to his home, and I run over to Mahir because I know I do not have much time. "Mahir, what was your papa talking to you about so seriously?" "Mama," he says in English. Being the oldest, he is so fluent in both languages. "There is nothing to worry about. Papa was telling me that some Americans are coming nearby to another village to give children medical care. He says that I will take the children to be seen and receive their shots. Malika will stay here to help you keep everything in order. There is nothing to worry about at all." Mahir pats me on the shoulder, and I am sickened at how much he looks like his father but has a kind heart, unlike his father.

Americans are coming to a nearby village? My heart begins to quicken. We have not had Americans in these parts of Iraq in years. I have to stay calm and focused. I cannot let him know that I know about this. I tell Mahir not to worry his papa with our conversation; there is no need for him to know that I know. I finish cleaning up the meal and get the children ready for bed. For once, I will go to bed with hopeful thoughts, thoughts that maybe, this nightmare will be over.

Chapter Two

TARA

～

"You know you don't have to do this." Tara's dad was leaning against the wall just inside her room as she finished packing up the last few items in her duffle bag. She paused and stared at him for a moment, and for the first time, truly began to see all the stress and worries from the years had caught up to him. The subtle wrinkles around his eyes, the permanent bags under his eyes that he swears is not from lack of sleep. She walked over to him and gave him a light jab in his ribs. "Dad, you know I have to do this. You know how much this means to me."

Tara's dad picks up an old faded picture that she is on the shelf near where he is standing. He rubs his finger over the woman in the frame, "God, you look so much like her. Not just on the outside, you are as fearless as she was." He pauses and takes a deep breath in. "I know you have to go. I just don't want you to get in over your head. I know you say this isn't about finding her, but we both know it is." Tara grabs the picture from her dad and looks at the picture. It's truly like looking into a mirror. The person smiling back at Tara has the same green eyes, same blonde hair, and the same heartwarming smile. The only difference is that Tara barely knew the person in the picture. Emily Sanders had been missing for close to fifteen years. Tara was just a toddler with blurry memories of her mom. She remembers the smile and her hugs, but more than that, it's just the stories her dad and family have shared with her over the years.

"I love you, dad. I promise you this is not just about finding out more about mom. I truly feel a calling to help people. I know this is where I need to be." And with that,

Tara's dad, Josh, gives her a big hug. "I love you too, Tara." Josh walks out before Tara can see the tears on his cheeks.

Tara takes the faded picture of her mom and adds it to her backpack. She has the photo memorized, but deep down, she hopes that she will need it to help look for her. Tara's primary job as a medic is to support villages in third-world countries. Tara's decision to take a break from med school was a difficult decision to make. Still, she couldn't pass up the opportunity to help local Iraq children get their vaccinations and ensure they were healthy enough to attend school. It was a bonus that the main town and surrounding villages where she would be working happened to be the last known area her mother had been seen alive.

Tara checks her phone and realizes that it's time to go. She grabs her duffle and her backpack and heads downstairs. Her dad is sitting at the kitchen table, staring blankly into his coffee. "I'll call you as soon as I can, dad. I promise." "I know. Tara, please be safe. I know they say it's safe now, but please, watch your back at all times." Tara gives him one more kiss on the forehead and heads out. Her not-so-little sister already said her goodbyes the day before. Alicia was on her missionary summer trip in Haiti and pretty much told her older sister, "I'll see you later."

As for Tara's stepmom, Dina, there wasn't much to say. Tara and Dina had never seen eye to eye. Dina disapproved of Tara's undying loyalty to her mom. She told Tara time and time again to accept that her mother was gone and should move on with her life.

Tara stepped out the back door and hopped into the back of the Uber, waiting for her. She didn't look back as they pulled away. She looked down at her wrist where she had the words 'Always Forward' tattooed in cursive on her right wrist, just like the one her mother had on her wrist. Tara was planning on meeting her fiancé at the airport, and from there, they would fly into Kuwait City to wait on a smaller plane to fly them into Baghdad. They would be escorted by private security to the village where they would live and work.

She was excited, anxious, and scared, all at once. She had no real plan on what to do if she found her mom. Her only plan was to get to Iraq, help the children, and do her best to find clues that would hopefully lead her to what happened to her mom.

She knew the Army's story, had memorized the report they had been given to her dad. She understood that after so many years, they had no choice but to declare her killed in action. Even though there was no proof and no remains, unlike one of the other soldier's remains found several years later. This was the final reason the Army declared Sergeant Emily Sanders deceased. But Tara clung to the fact that there was nobody or any proof that her mom was dead; that is why she still had hope. How could she know for sure that her mom was dead without any proof? The rest of the family had accepted it. Her little sister, Alicia, was only one year old when their mom had left; she never knew her. Her dad clung to hope for as long as he could, but raising two young daughters while being in the Army himself was not easy. Tara never felt bitterness or jealousy for her dad falling in love with Dina, but that didn't mean she would ever call Dina her mom or accept that her mom was gone. Deep down, Tara believed with all her heart that she was out there, and if the Army weren't going to continue to search for her, then she would do it herself.

Tara saw Nick before he saw her. How could she not notice him, a 6'5, with those dark brown curls she liked to tease him about. He swore his hair had been his good luck charm throughout pre-med school. He promised her he would chop it all off once he graduated and was a proper doctor. If this man wanted longer and luscious hair than her and was willing to put med school on hold to travel across the globe with her, then he was a keeper in her book.

"Hey baby, I didn't see you sneak up on me," Nick said as he gathered Tara up in his arms. Nick was from Northern Ohio and had gone home after they graduated from Clemson in May. With their upcoming trip with Red Cross, he wanted to spend a month with his family. They had agreed it was a great idea to spend time with family. Iraq was considered 'safe' for organizations like the American Red Cross, though there was always a chance they could be a victim of violence.

Tara squeezed him hard, "It's so good to see you. My nerves have been getting to me all week. I just want to get over there and get to work." Nick pulled apart from Tara, "To work for the Red Cross, right? Not just to find your mom? I know what you want to do, but remember, we have a JOB to do while we are there." Tara rolled her eyes; Nick and her dad were beginning to sound like the same person. "I know what we are there to do, but they can't work us 24 hours a day. I plan on snooping around on my own time."

"Flight 1462 to Kuwait City will begin to board in 15 minutes," a voice over the airport intercom announces. Both Tara and Nick grab their bags and make their way closer to the gate. Tara had to force herself not to sprint on the plane. In 24 hours, Tara would be in Kuwait City and one step closer to being in the same country as her mom.

When Tara and Nick landed in Kuwait, they were met by the sun's warmth; even though it was January, it could still get warm quickly during the day, but then, the temperatures quickly dropped once the sun went down. Tara knew that they would be in for some pretty hot days once they hit April and May.

Tara's dad, Josh, had served overseas in both Afghanistan and Iraq. As a Special Forces soldier, he had done ten (10) six-month combat deployments over his 20-year career. Tara valued the advice and tips he had given her, but she clearly did not think he was serious when he told her it's like walking into an oven. She squinted as they climbed down the stairs of the plane onto the airstrip. There was a bus waiting for them to hop on. Once they were on the bus, Tara learned that fifteen other volunteers were headed to Kuwait to make the final trek into Iraq.

The plan was to spend a week in Kuwait City, getting acclimated to the heat and attending several trainings on the culture. They had already gone through extensive training back in the states and had to receive more vaccinations than Tara had ever remembered getting as a child. Her dad reassured her they were all necessary and made sure she took her malaria pills like a good little Army brat.

Tara didn't feel the jet lag so many people warned her about. Growing up as an Army brat meant they moved around every 2-3 years. Tara was used to going from one side of the country to the other and even spending two years in Germany.

They loaded the bus and sat down shoulder to shoulder in their seats. "Psst," Nick whispers in Tara's ear, "there's no AC on this bus." "Way to go, Captain Obvious," Tara chuckles back to him. "You may just have to chop off those auburn locks of yours before the year is up." "No way, little lady. I will spot a man-bun that you have never seen before I chop off these locks," Nick says as he flips his hair in Tara's face.

The ride from the airport to their hotel in Kuwait City takes close to an hour due to traffic. When they get to the hotel, Tara is confident she has dropped ten pounds from sweating.

"If I keep sweating like this, I will melt away before we even make it to the village," she says as she tries to find a dry part of her shirt to pat her face with. The volunteers exit the bus and make their way into the hotel. Tara's dad had told her how this was the hotel that the Iraqi Army had used during the invasion of Kuwait in the '90s. Looking around now, you would never know that this location had been the host to such an evil regime.

Once they entered the hotel lobby, they were greeted by the air conditioning system. All fifteen (15) of the volunteers sighed in unison. They followed a sign in the lobby into a smaller ballroom off the lobby. There were tables at the entrance with American Red Cross volunteers ready to check in the new volunteers and get them situated. Even though Nick and Tara were planning on getting married in two years and already lived together, they were not allowed to stay in the same hotel room. They each got in lines assigned by the first letter of their last names. Nick went to the left for line A-D while Tara went to the right to find the line for S-V.

Tara got her passport and immunization records out of her bag as she approached the table. She handed her documents over to the volunteer. "Ms. Tara Sanders, welcome to Kuwait," said the volunteer handling her documentation. "Thank you, I am excited to get to work," Tara said as she smiled at the volunteer. The volunteer looked up over his glasses, "Look, this mission may sound like fun and games, but remember, Iraq has seen a lot of bloodshed and turmoil. Don't forget where you are at and what you are here to do."

Tara was shocked by how serious the volunteer got so quickly. She stammered to respond, "I didn't mean any offense. I understand the severity of what we are headed into. I guess excited was a bad choice of words. I am eager to begin helping the kids in the villages." The volunteer stamped a few documents and handed everything back to Tara without looking up but said, "Go ahead to the next table behind me, and they will get you your room key and maps of the area."

Tara grabbed her papers and continued. She didn't even bother saying, 'thank you' to the volunteer. Clearly, he was done with her, and she hoped she wouldn't cross his path again.

The rest of the afternoon was spent getting unpacked and cleaned up for dinner. After dinner, they would have their welcome session.

Tara knew once they got to Iraq, a simple shower would be a rare commodity. She took the coolest shower and reveled in the feel of it. She wondered if her mom had running water or the ability to shower. She knew thinking like this was dangerous and should expect the worst, but she needed to believe she was alive. She needed to be vigilant once she got to her assigned village. Otherwise, what was the point in even being here.

She met Nick in the lobby, and they headed back to the same ballroom they had been in earlier.

Nick moaned when he caught a whiff of the food. "Ugh, they really are serving us traditional local food...." "Um yeah... suck it up, buttercup. My dad has been telling you that you would have to open up your food horizons for months. I'm sure you will find something to eat." Patting his stomach, Nick replies, "Damn right, I'm a growing boy. I can't starve while I'm here. My hair may stop growing."

Tara rolled her eyes and pulled Nick into the ballroom. They found their seats at a table towards the front of the room. There were already three other people sitting at their table- one female and two males. The girl was stunning with piercing blue eyes, fair skin, and long jet-black hair. She stood up, came over, and gave Tara and Nick big hugs. "Hi, there!! I'm Rosie! Since you two are the last ones here, I'm going to guess you are Tara and Nick?" Tara immediately felt at ease and could tell her and Rosie would hit it off. Tara shrugged and smiled at the group, "Yeah, I guess we are the stragglers," Tara said as they all took their seats. The other two at the table waved and introduced themselves. Jake and Sean were both from upstate New York, also taking a year off before beginning Med School. Rosita, or as she liked to be called Rosie, was a bonafide free spirit. She had tried college, but after one semester, gave it all up. She had spent the last several years volunteering in Africa with another non-profit organization before deciding to come on board with the Red Cross.

Throughout the rest of the first evening in Kuwait, the team of volunteers listened to speakers from the local Red Cross chapters and the lead organizer from the states. They were given the rest of the evening to settle in and relax. The rest of the week would be a whirlwind of training and final preparations for their trip into Iraq.

Tara had been training for this trip most of her life. She never accepted that her mother was dead, and from as far back as she could remember, she knew she would make her way to Iraq one day. As the week stretched on, Tara tried to focus on what they were telling the volunteers. The Do's and Don'ts, what to expect, and on and on. She had begun to study Arabic in middle school, used to have her dad quiz her when he was home between his deployments to the Middle East. He used to tell her, "Tara, enough is enough. You know you are better at speaking Arabic than I am. Leave it alone!" Little did he know what her ulterior motives were for learning the language and everything there was to know about the various cultures and religions of Iraq.

By the time she was thirteen, she knew she wanted to become a doctor with the primary intent to work in Iraq. She wanted to help those left behind to survive after decades of being at war but also wanted to find her mother.

The last night in Kuwait, Tara couldn't sleep. All she could think about was her mother and what her life would have been like if she had never been captured. She took the faded photo of her mother out of her journal and stared at the smiling woman looking back at her. "I know you're out there somewhere, mom, and I am going to find you one way or another."

Chapter Three

JOSH

J osh watched Tara drive off in her Uber. He had talked this day through with his therapist, and they had agreed that he would keep it together for Tara. God, she reminded him so much of Emily; it literally made his heart hurt. It wasn't enough for Tara to be Emily's twin, but her tenacity and stubbornness were all Emily's too. Josh walked around Tara's room, even though she barely lived at home anymore. She used his house as a landing pad for holidays and summer breaks. He hardly ever had a reason to come in here, but now he didn't want to leave. He sat down on the edge of her bed and looked at all the trophies and plaques she had won over the years. Not only was she exceptionally gifted with her academics, which was proof with all the science fair awards, but she was athletic as well. He smiled and liked to think that she got her skills on the basketball court from him.

He got up and began walking to the door and paused when he caught a glimpse of an old faded and frayed yellow ribbon. It's the one that Emily had pinned to Tara's dress the day Emily was leaving. He reached out and gently touched it, not wanting to disrupt its spot on the shelf. He had been so confident that Emily's mission would be safe. He had just completed a six-month tour in Afghanistan and had been in some intense situations. He hadn't shared any of that with Emily since she gave birth to Alicia shortly after he had come home. Alicia was barely five months old when Emily received her orders for deployment. She was such a mess, still dealing with post-partum depression and now the guilt that she would have to leave her toddler and baby behind. Josh had to keep it together and convinced her that everything would be fine and Alicia wouldn't even remember her being gone.

Josh pounded his fist into the door jamb, hating himself for not trying harder to keep her home. God, he knew today would stir up some emotions, but he hadn't prepared himself for all the guilt to come flooding back in again.

For once, Josh was grateful Dina was at work. Dina and Tara hadn't had the best stepmom/step-daughter relationship, and Dina had claimed she couldn't get the day off from work. Josh closed Tara's room up and headed for his shed outside. He opened up his workspace, where he stored all his tools and yard equipment. Since retiring from the military, he had to find hobbies, and what do you know? He loved tinkering around and keeping his yard pristine. He walked to the back of the shed, where he kept an old aluminum cabinet. He opened it up and brought out a Rubbermaid tote. He kept his most sacred memories of Emily in this box out here because he felt like he was betraying his marriage to Dina if he kept any of them in the house.

He slowly opened up the tote and took a deep breath. He hadn't looked at anything in there since they had buried the empty casket all those years ago. As he flipped through their wedding photos, Josh smiled as he looked at a twenty-two-year-old Josh and a barely twenty-one-year-old Emily. They had a typical military wedding at the courthouse with Emily wearing a simple sundress and Josh in his collared shirt and khakis. They were beaming at the camera, so young and so in love. He kept moving along through the photos and stopped at one of Emily holding Tara in the hospital. If he had thought he had an undying love for Emily before, he had discovered a whole new level of love when he watched her give birth to Tara. She was a complete champ on the delivery table, with no painkillers at all. Looking at the photo reminded him of all the promises they both had made to Tara that day. He set the picture down and wiped his eyes. He knew this might not be the best thing to do, but he just needed a few more minutes reliving how their lives had started.

The final item he pulled out of the tote was a letter addressed from Emily to Josh, dated a week before she went missing. He received it the day after the phone call came in to inform him that she was missing in action, along with her medic, Specialist Grant. He knew it wasn't healthy to read this letter, and it's not like it wasn't engrained in his memory from the millions of times he had read it in those early years. He gently slipped it out of the envelope all the same and unfolded it to see her beautiful penmanship.

My Dearest Josh,

I hope you are surviving Alicia's teething! In the last letter I received from you; I could tell you were a bit frazzled. I REALLY hope you were kidding about rubbing whiskey on her gums. We don't need an infant alcoholic on our hands! All kidding aside, I know you are doing an amazing job of being the best dad in the entire universe to both our girls. They are the luckiest kids alive, and I am the luckiest woman alive to have you as my better half.

We are all settled in nowhere at Anaconda. It's brutally hot, just like you said it would be, and I have debated going full GI Jane and shaving all my hair off, but for now, I will keep it as is. I must say, I don't think I will ever get used to burning my crap. That literally is the foulest smell ever! But we don't really have many other options out here.

We have been doing some basic runs to some surrounding areas. (You know OPSEC won't let me share where with you, although I have a feeling you will follow up with your people on this.) We haven't had too many issues yet on missions; a few random gunshots, and every once in a while, we hear an explosion off in the distance. But, most of the major issues are done with. Some of our guys even feel safe enough not to wear their flak vest when we are outside the wire. Don't worry though, this mama is wearing her shit! I am not about to get hit with a stray bullet to the chest.

I do have to say that I miss you and the girls terribly. I try so hard to turn off my emotions for you all, but it's hard. My milk finally dried up, which has helped, but the nights are the hardest for me. I lay on my cot, and when I close my eyes, I can see you and the girls standing there as I walked away, and it breaks my heart all over again.

I know I have too much time left in this country to begin a countdown, but I am only ten months and 24 days until I can see you and our girls again.

I love you with everything in me, Josh Sanders. And remember, the only way we can go is always forward. So, we both have to stay strong and stay focused on our missions in front of us.

Until next time my love,

Your sweetheart- Emily

Josh gently refolded the letter back up and slid it into the envelope it had arrived in all those years ago. *Until next time my love.* That was the line he must have reread over and over again, for days and weeks after he had gotten the news. There was never a next time. If it hadn't been for their girls, he would have killed himself for sure. The grief of losing Emily, his first love, had been more than he could handle, but he had to remain strong for Tara and Alicia. They needed him, but he needed them probably even more.

Josh packed up the tote and gave it one last tap before placing it back in its spot in the cabinet. He decided he needed to check out the noise the lawnmower had made on his last cruise around the yard. This would be a good distraction for him until Dina came home from work later. It was way healthier than grabbing a drink and wallowing even more in the past, plus, he had to remember Emily's motto- always forward. She used to say it for everything, but she wasn't wrong. The only way to go was forward; you can't go back in time. So, even though he held on to memories from their life together, he knew his life was here in the present, and he could only move forward.

Chapter Four

TARA

~

The heat of the August sun is unforgiving to everyone, even the medics inside the makeshift tent. By now, Tara thought for sure she would be used to the heat, but after several months of working in the summer heat of Iraq, she was nowhere closer to being acclimated to the oven they were living and working in.

The morning had been steady, and word had been spreading in the surrounding villages about the med station near Mosul. She had lost count after twenty-five (25) children, and the heat was beginning to play tricks on her. "Hey, Tara," Rosita came up behind Tara and placed a slightly cooler than oven temperature water bottle in her hands. "You need to drink more water. You are sweating like a banshee and haven't had a break yet."

"Thank you, Mama Rosie," Tara said as she grabbed the water and slammed it down in one gulp.

"I'm good though, seriously. I just want to get these kids through as fast as possible. I feel terrible for all the ones standing in the blazing sun. At least in here, we are shaded." "Suit yourself then. I am going to see if I can find something to eat. I'll bring you back what I can." And with that, Rosita walked out of the tent, leaving Tara as the only medic left on duty.

"Ummmm, okay, not exactly what I was thinking she was going to do, but the show must go on," Tara muttered under her breath as she waved in the next group of children. A taller boy walked into the tent with a parade of children behind him. He couldn't have been more than 13 or 14, yet his eyes looked so old. She greeted him in the native tongue, "Good afternoon. I hope you have travelled here safely today." The young boy with old eyes replied in near-perfect English, "You do not have to trouble yourself with Arabic. My siblings and I are well versed in English."

Tara was taken aback for a moment. She had been dealing with Iraqi children for close to eight months now, and not one child or adult for that matter could barely speak English. Some could sputter out a few words but never complete sentences like this young man. "My apologies, sir. I am not used to speaking in English while I work." Tara said. "I see you have quite the gathering with you today," Tara winked at one of the younger children hiding behind the young man.

"Ah, yes. These are a few of my siblings. I could not bring them all in one day. The younger ones tend to do a lot of work on these long walks." The young man pats the girl hiding behind him on the head. "Well, I am Tara, and I promise to get you and your siblings through as quickly as possible. Once you finish in here, the next tent will have some snacks and water for you all on your trip back home."

The young man gave Tara a nod and turned around to gather the rest of his family. Tara begins getting the immunizations ready along with a notecard to document the family. "If you don't mind, can I have you and your siblings' names?" Tara asked the young man. "Um, yes, my name is Mahir, and these two young ladies are Ashya and Abya." Two identical twins come forward with their heads down.

"Hi Ashya and Abya, I'm Tara. I know this may be a little scary, but I promise I am here to help you, so you don't get sick in the future." Tara gently grabbed each one of their hands while she got them to look at her. Tara was frozen in time. When the girls looked at her, it was like looking at her little sister Alicia. If the girls had green eyes and blonde hair, there would be no difference at all. Tara blinked a few times, thinking she must be more home sick than she thought. She went back to getting the girls prepped for their shots.

"Mahir, have you or any of your siblings ever received a shot before?" Tara asked Mahir as she rolled Ashya's sleeves up. "No, but our mother has instructed us about it.

She received them when she was a child. She said there is nothing to be afraid of, and it will only hurt for a moment."

"Ahhh, your mother is a wise woman. Why did she not travel with you all today? Adults can also receive these booster shots." Tara finished with Ashya, putting a SpongeBob Band-Aid on the spot where she had just poked her.

"Ummmm," Mahir stammered, which considering how well he spoke English, Tara found a little strange.

"She does not travel outside of our village. She......ummmmm...."

Tara could tell Mahir was uncomfortable talking about his mother, so she changed the subject as she moved on to Abya. "It's okay, Mahir, you don't have to answer. How about we talk about the snacks in the next tent. Have you all ever had fruit by the foot?" Tara asked with an extra bounce of enthusiasm. Both girls' eyes got big, and they shook their heads, meaning no. "Well," Tara said with a laugh, "You all are in for a treat! Fruit by the foot is like eating a whole bunch of fruit but in flat, candy, sugary goodness form!" Tara poked Abya in the arm and then head-butted her lightly, which made both girls giggle.

After Tara finished with the twins, another young man, not much younger than Mahir, came forward.

"I am Maimun, Mahir's brother." The young man had bold black eyes and a presence that exerted strength and leadership. "It's very nice to meet you, Maimun. Go ahead and roll up your sleeve for me." Tara said to Maimun as she prepared another set of shots for this young man. Tara could tell Maimun was the serious one and wasn't sure if he was up for small talk. "Mahir and Maimun, do you two have any hobbies or past times you enjoy?"

"Umm, we do not have time for hobbies, as you call them. We attend school, and when we are not working on our studies, we are with our father learning his business." Mahir replies before Maimun has a chance to answer. The brothers steal a glance at each other, and Tara senses something is being shared between the brothers. She knew this all too well from millions of exchanges with her sister Alicia. "Well, I am sure your father appreciates you two helping him and learning the family business." Again, Tara knew not to pry. She wanted to learn more about this family of Iraqi children that were fluent in Arabic and English, but she knew her place in this country as well. She had to respect traditions and the overall view of females.

"Mahir, do you write in English as well as you speak it?" Tara asked as she wiped his arm off with an alcohol wipe. "Not too well. I can print, but I cannot write in cursive." Mahir's cheeks began to redden as if not knowing cursive was such a bad thing. "Oh well, most Americans can't even write in cursive! Don't feel bad about that at all." Tara handed Mahir a notecard. "Do you mind writing down all your names and ages for me? And I know you may not have an address as we do in America, but can you write down your village and family name?"

"Sure, I can do that for you. But why do you need this?" Mahir hesitantly takes the pencil and notecard. "This is how we keep track of how many people we help each day. Plus, if you or your siblings have any allergic reactions, we can look back and see what shots you had." Mahir nodded and began printing their names on the card. Tara began to clean up for the next group and decided to see what else she could learn from this young man with such old eyes.

"Mahir, who taught you and your siblings such good English?" Mahir froze in mid printing of 'Abya.' He never took his eyes off the card. "Our father. Our father taught us." Tara nodded, not believing that for a minute. "Oh, that makes sense. I'm sure your father is a wise man. I mean, he brought you all this way today since your mother couldn't make the trek." Mahir finished up printing all the information and handed the card back over to Tara.

"I brought my siblings here on my own. My father is an important man in our village. He cannot be worried about taking care of children." And with that, Tara knew the conversation was over. She took the card from Mahir and gave him a weak smile. She waved at the children, and Mahir escorted them out of the back side of the tent to collect their snacks in the next tent. Tara folded up the notecard and put it in her cargo pocket. She was not done with Mahir Baz just yet. There was more to learn about him and his siblings.

As the day came to a close, Tara packed up her med station, disposing of all the trash and stocking up on supplies for the next day. She was working on an idea that would allow her to gain more access to Mahir and his family. Just as she was packing up and getting ready to walk back to the main medical tent, Doc, as everyone called him, came walking by Tara.

"DOC! Just the person I need to talk to." Tara ran up to Doc, whose real name was Doctor Ferrero, but for short, everyone just called him Doc. Doc had been leading these volunteer missions for the past decade. He was a retired Army doctor and felt a calling to continue working with villages in Iraq once he retired. His wife, Nurse Sue, supported his vision and passion for helping families in Iraq. She managed all the logistics of working with several non-profits like the Red Cross to ensure they always had the best-skilled volunteers on hand for the yearlong missions.

Doc stopped in his tracks and looked up over his bi-focal. He swore his eyesight was fine but that the glasses were just to 'help make things crisper' since he was always in a hurry. "Oh, hello Tara, another busy day today. I am still tallying up the totals, but I think we saw close to 100 children today. Our biggest day yet! Word is spreading about us being here." "Wow, Doc! That is great news!! Yes, today was definitely a busy and hot one, which is perfect for the proposition I want to run past you." Tara tilted her head and gave Doc her sweet half-smile that always seemed to work on her dad when she wanted to get her way.

"You've got 60 seconds to pitch me whatever crazy idea you have now," Doc said as he walked under the shade of her work tent. "Geez, you make it seem like I have had SO many crazy ideas. I mean, the food requests weren't even for me; those were for Nick." Tara crossed her arms and blocked Doc's way out, so he now had no choice but to hear her out. "Okay, two minutes- GO!" Doc looked back down at his clipboard, and Tara knew she shouldn't push it too much further.

Tara began to pace in front of Doc as she spoke, "So, we both can agree that the number of children and families we see daily is picking up. However, there are only several of us that are fully capable of understanding the local Arabic dialect. I know for me, I have been pulled away from my line of kids to assist with translations for another medic."

"Alright, we can agree on this point. You have my full attention now." Doc folds his arms and tucks his clipboard under his arm. His stare is intense, and Tara gets nervous; she won't confidently say what she wants to say. But then she catches a glimpse of her tattoo on her wrist and knows there is only one way to go, always forward. "What if I told you that I met not one but two local teenage boys that spoke English probably better than most American citizens? What if we could pay them a minimal amount to assist with translating for the medics that seem to struggle the most with the locals?" Tara paused and stopped pacing. She knew that Doc needed to process what she had just said. He was an extremely analytical thinker, and if she pushed too hard, he would just walk away.

"Okay..." Doc said, but Tara knew this was not the permission 'okay.' This was the 'I'm still processing what you said, OKAY.' "Hypothetically speaking, if we could get these two boys to work for us, what makes you think they will want to?" Tara knew Doc would pose a question like this, but she was ready. "Their father is a businessman; he already has the boys working with him to learn whatever it is their family business is. I think that both boys would see the benefit of earning their own money and showing their father they can provide as well. We both know how important the male sons are in these villages. These boys brought two of their younger siblings today but mentioned there were more at home. I'm not a betting woman, but I bet they can use some extra money in their household." And with that, Tara went back to pacing.

"Well, you know I have to run it by the true boss around here. Nurse Sue will have to crunch some numbers and determine what we can afford to pay them, IF we can even pay them with actual money. We may have to pay them with supplies from time to time." Doc shifted his stance and was beginning to stare ahead, and Tara could tell he was on her side. "So, you're saying there's a chance we could hire these two boys?" Tara was trying not to jump up and down like she did when she was eight and had just got her way with her dad.

"Well, hold on now. I'm not saying yes just yet. As I said, let me talk to the head honcho, and I will let you know tomorrow." Doc started to leave the tent, and Tara reached out and grabbed his arm.

"Thank you, Doc., I know Nurse Sue will agree this would be worth the investment. Just think of how many more families we could see daily if there wasn't a language barrier." And with that, Doc nodded and walked off towards the main tent. Tara finished packing up her supplies and followed behind Doc with a revived surge of energy.

Chapter Five

EMILY

"**S**anders! Goddammit! Sanders! Answer me now!!"
I hear Specialist Rodriguez screaming my name. I want to respond; I really do. But I can't get my mouth to work. There is so much pressure on my head. Why does it feel like everything is crushing my head? And why is it so hot? It's like I am on fire. Why do I feel like that?

"SANDERS!!!! ANSWER ME, GODDAMMIT!!" I feel a tug on my arm, and I tell myself to try.

I try. I try so hard, but my eyes and mouth are like they are sewn shut. How do I get them to move?

"OH SHIT! WE GOTTA GO, RODRIGUEZ!" I hear another soldier screaming. Is that Simmons? I can't tell for sure. I think its Simmons.

"WE CAN'T LEAVE THEM HERE!" Rodriguez tugs on my arm again, and I try to move. But nothing happens. How can I hear them and not be able to move or speak?

"IF WE STAY HERE, WE WILL BE AS DEAD AS THE REST OF THEM. IT'S TIME TO MOVE!" Yes, that is Simmons yelling now. I can hear that southern twang coming out in his yelling that he swears isn't there. The tugging on my arm stops. I don't hear any more voices...

No, no, no, no.... Where is everyone going? Please, don't leave me here. Don't leave!! I swear I am alive! I can hear you; I just can't get my mouth to work!

gunfire so much gunfire. What is going on? And the heat! The heat is moving up my body!

No, no, no, no!! Where are my people? Why can't I use my arms? This isn't right. This isn't what should be happening. We have trained for this. Where are my people? Why aren't they coming for me?

WHY IS IT SO DAMN HOT?????

There are nights that he leaves me alone. These are the nights I try to put memories back in order in my mind. I remember being in the Humvee when we were on a routine mission back to camp and had been joking around about something. I know this because when I picture myself in the A-driver's seat, I am happy, but I cannot for the life of me remember what we were laughing about. I have the hand mic wedged between my Kevlar strap and my ear, so I don't have to hold it there. I have the window down to the Humvee, and I am trying desperately to get some airflow up the sleeve of my ACU's. Even though it is 21:30, it so still stifling hot out for May. My driver, Specialist Rodriguez, must have been telling me a joke. But the next memory I have is the roar of the explosion. It felt like the ground had split open. One minute I was laughing, and the next moment, I have no idea what was going on.

It has taken me so long to piece this together. I haven't had any medical treatment since being captured, but I am certain besides my physical injuries, I must have sustained head trauma. The migraines I still get to this day completely immobilize me; I can barely breathe when one of the migraine attacks hits me. He used to beat me when these would ensue. He thought I was pretending and would tell me that if he beat me, surely that would make the pain go away. In the early days, I would fight, scratch, and do whatever I could to hurt him. I used to fight back, but this only made my punishments much longer. Eventually, my spirit was broken; somewhere along the way, I lost my spirit completely.

I go back to that night. After the explosion, I remember feeling like we were flying. But soon enough, the flying turned into crashing. If I had to guess, from the way I felt when I woke up, we must have been blown off the ground and landed upside down.

That would explain all the pressure I felt on my head and neck. This is where things still do not make sense. All the years that have gone by, all the days and nights to try to put it all back together, but this is where I can only remember spurts of what happened. Sometimes, I think this is what brings on my migraines. I try so hard to remember, but my brain is blocking it. A searing pain will strike, usually above my right eye. I rub this spot and feel the indent that is permanently there. I haven't seen myself in a mirror in ages, but I assume the indent was caused by something slicing my forehead. It could have been shrapnel or from going airborne and landing on my head. Either way, the migraines usually start here, or the pain shoots right into my skull. I can't see, I can't hear, and I can't talk when the pain hits. I grab my head and squeeze as hard as I can to relieve the pressure. Sometimes this works, but most of the time, it does not. Sometimes, my legs still feel like they are on fire. I pull up my dress or what one would more than likely call rags and look at the scars. I remember those first few weeks after the explosion. The pain was beyond intense; I was sure I would need both legs amputated, but somehow, I survived.

Due to the scarring on my legs, I can't walk very well. I need a cane most days just to walk outside. I'm not exactly sure what the villagers have been told about me or where I came from, but they know I am a prisoner. They also know never to question Mohammad Baz. He is one of the senior elders of this village, and everyone fears him.

Over the years, the children I have given birth to have asked so many questions about me. "Why is your skin so much lighter than our skin?" "Why are your eyes that shade of green?" "Why do you have words written on your skin?" "Why can't you understand Arabic?" As the years have gone by, the older children educate the younger ones, so the questions have slowed down. He doesn't like it when they inquire about where I came from, and I learned a very long time ago to keep what I can remember to myself.

I am woken up to the sounds of Asad crying in his makeshift crib next to my mat on the dirt floor. I can tell it will be another blistering hot day. It can't be more than 6:00 in the morning, and the sun is already up and shedding its rays across the village. I take a deep breath and close my eyes. Asad is still crying, and I hear footsteps coming over to me. I open my eyes and see Mohammad- the man, the monster that has kept me captive here for all these years.

He stands over me, hands on his hips, "Are you going to get up and tend to the baby? Or do I need to remind you how lucky you are to have been given another day with us?" He continues to stand there and wait for my reaction. I roll over to my side and push myself up. As I roll into a sitting position, every movement brings pain to my body. I try to hide the grimace, but nothing escapes Mohammad. He takes the grimace as a sign of defiance and leans downs, and slaps me across the face. Asad continues to wail, drawing in the older children. Malika runs over to pick up Asad. Mohammad puts his left arm out to stop her. "DO. NOT. TOUCH. THE. BABY." He says slowly, meanwhile never taking his eyes off me.

Malika walks backwards back to the doorway with her older brothers Mahir and Maimun.

"GET. UP. WOMAN." The monster raises his voice even more. Asad is now to the point of holding his breath between wails. I move, my face now throbbing from where he struck me. I somehow find the strength to stand and pick up the sweet baby, who has no idea of the world he has been brought into. Mohammad, pleased with my compliance, turns and walks away, shelling out commands to the older children in Arabic. I sit back down with Asad and begin to nurse him. He immediately begins to calm down, and I stare out the open window at the blazing sun.

Malika quietly comes back into the room and kneels next to Asad and me. She hands me a small wet rag to wipe my face with. I hadn't even noticed I was weeping. I take what is given to me and begin to wipe my face. "Mama, please do not try to be fearless with Papa."

Interestingly, Malika also thought my struggles at sitting up was an act of defiance. He has begun to brainwash the older children like he did to the villagers; that I am the defiant one. They truly have no clue how much pain I am in. I hand the rag back to her and pat her on the cheek. There are no words that I can speak freely that will not be taken out of context. Malika bows her head and leaves as quietly as she came in. I continue to nurse Asad until he falls back to sleep. I gently lay him down next to me on his makeshift bed. I know I need to get up and begin my morning chores, but the morning's commotion has made me more exhausted than I am after a full day's work.

The next thing I know, my sweet chubby, green-eyed son, Khayru, is tapping me on the shoulder. I open my arms, and he crawls into the opposite crook of my arm from his baby brother, Asad. I keep praying that since both my youngest boys and my youngest daughter have green eyes that this is a sign that they have more of my spirit within them than their father's. Khayra turns his head to the side and reaches up to kiss my cheek. I squeeze both the boys and find the strength to begin our day.

Lulu comes in and helps me with Asad. Even though she is only seven, she is such a help to me with the youngest two boys. She helps entertain them while I begin my morning chores. I tend to pour buckets of waste, taking them to the farthest part of our property to begin our burn pile for the day. Once I have the fire contained, I begin to prepare breakfast for the younger children. The older children- Mahir, Maimun, Malika, and now Abya and Ashya have already left for school. The youngest three stay with me, and we eat our modest breakfast of rice with saffron from our garden. We have just enough water to have a few sips each until the oldest come home later.

When the older children come home later in the day, they huddle together, talking in hushed tones. The younger kids and I sit up against our hut, trying to stay in what shade we have available. "Hello there," I say to them as they approach. "You all look like you are either plotting something good or something terribly bad." I smile because the twins begin to giggle, and Abya pulls something out of her book bag.

"Here, Mama, we picked you up a gift on our way home from school! Open it! Open it!" Abya and her sister Ashya are jumping up and down, synchronized, like everything they do.

I tilt my head to the left and stare puzzled at the oldest two- Mahir and Maimun. "How were you able to pick me up a gift? There is no money for things like this?" I asked them, puzzled and concerned about accepting any gift with fear of what onslaught it would bring on later.

Mahir stands up a little straighter and says in a voice just like his father's, "I have been picking up small jobs for some of the elders in the village. Maimun and I have begun translating for some of the families that are visiting the clinic. The clinic pays us what they can." Abya leans down and places the small brown paper gift in my hands. My eyes begin to water even though I have no idea what is inside the wrapping. It's the thought that these children, who were all born out of pure evil, can be so loving. I look up at each of them, and even though my monster can be seen in each one of them, there are slight similarities with me. Mahir and Maimun both have my dimple on their chin, and until they begin to grow their beards, I take joy in seeing this. Malika has my cheekbones, and the twins both have a sense of joy in everything they do, similar to what my true oldest daughter once had.

Before I begin to cry in front of them and their father arrives home from his work, I quickly unwrap the small package. Inside the wrapping is a clear quartz stone, no bigger than the inside of the palm of my hand. I take it out of the wrapper and squeeze it tightly. "It is known as the master healer," Maimun says. "We all know how much pain you are in, even though we know you try to hide it from us. We don't know how to make him stop treating you that way, but we hope that this stone will bring you some relief."

At that, I begin to weep heavily. I can't even try to hide it any longer. I have not been given any sort of true gift in so long. Having not one but five of my children have such deep compassion brings up so many emotions inside me. Lulu, who has been sitting next to me this entire time with Asad in her lap, begins to rub my back. I do have allies here, after all. I may have been raped and violently beaten to conceive each one of these children, but they still have good in their souls. I finally get my emotions under control, and I find the words to thank them. I then tell them that this must remain our secret. Their father can never know about their generosity towards me. All the children, even the baby Asad nod their heads in agreement. This moment will become the beginning of a true secret pact between these innocent souls and myself.

Chapter Six

TARA

"Mahir!! Wait up!!" Tara jogs over to Mahir and his brother Maimun. It's the end of yet another blistering hot day, yet these two barely looked phased by the heat. "Hello, Miss Tara." Mahir gently bows his head as he greets Tara. Maimun, the younger one, keeps his eyes averted from Tara. She doesn't think it's because he is nervous around her but more so out of respect that she is a single female. He seems to be the one that follows their customs very strictly.

Tara catches her breath and places her hands on her hips. "I haven't had time to catch up with you two since you began working with us. I can't express my gratitude enough for all your help. Having the two of you help with translating is allowing us to help even more kids and families." The boys look at each other, and Mahir responds, "Truly, it is us that should be thanking you. By allowing us to work here, we are able to help provide for our family. You have no idea what that means to us." Again, Mahir gently bowed his head to Tara. "Now, you must excuse us, we cannot be late for our family dinner." And with that, Mahir and Maimun turned to walk away.

Tara still had not met the rest of their family, and she was dying to learn more about his other siblings and his mother that could not leave their village. "You know Mahir, if the rest of your family are not able to make the trek here to receive their shots, I'm sure we could arrange to do a visit to your village. I would hate for the rest of your family not to receive their immunizations. Especially your mother, if she has any more children, it would help her and any future children she has of contracting any illnesses." Tara smiled and internally was screaming for him to agree. "Miss Tara, that is a very kind offer. I would have to ask my father and the other elders' permission to bring anyone outside into our village. That is not up to either one of us." Mahir gave her a weak smile, and before she could reply, they turned again and began to walk quickly away.

She knew she might have pushed too hard, but she had to plant the seed. This would at least get Mahir thinking about it, and who knows, maybe he would discuss it with his father after all. She knew she had to be patient and wait it out. She had kept her true mission a secret still. She had learned from over hearing other locals talk in line that the area they were in was still known to house underground insurgent armies. She knew if she began being vocal about searching for her mother, it would only be a matter of time before receiving some backlash.

That night after dinner, she decided to make her one weekly call home to her dad. He was the one person she could be open and raw with. Josh had completed so many tours in the Middle East and was exposed to more trauma than Tara could ever comprehend. Josh answered after the third ring, knowing that the international number could only be one of his two daughters. "Dear daddy," Tara said as if she was still ten and it was him calling her from overseas. "Well, hello there, long-lost daughter from the far east. I got used to only hearing from my daughter in the Caribbean." Josh chuckled at his own ridicule of his oldest daughter. He really couldn't be surprised that both his daughters had chosen professions that led them to third-world war countries to help others. "I know, I know. I don't call home enough. But at least you know if something bad would happen, you would know right away." As soon as the words left her mouth, Tara felt terrible for saying them. But Josh took it in strides. "Roger that, Tara. So how is it going out there? Are you surviving the heat?"

Tara rolled her eyes as she wiped more sweat from her forehead. "Surviving is a nice way to put it. I'm getting by, how about that? I know you told me it would be unbearable, but this is beyond unbearable!"

"You can't say I didn't warn you. I told you it was like sticking your head in the oven set at 500 degrees." Josh again begins to chuckle at his own joke. "How is Nick holding on? He cut all those locks yet?"

"NO WAY!! He's suffering, though, I can tell. But I barely even see him since we are on opposite sides of the medical village. They have him and the other male medics working directly just with the older men that come in." Tara paused, not sure if she should share with her dad her suspicions just yet. She still didn't have a lot to go on, but her gut told her that she was on the right track. "Dad," she pauses again and then decides to go for it. "What if I told you, I think I might have a lead on mom?"

"Tara bug," This is what Josh had called her ever since she could remember. When he used this term of endearment, it usually meant a lecture of some sort was on the horizon. "I thought we went over this before you left. You can't get sucked into conspiracy theories or half-cocked ideas because your gut is telling you something. You could get yourself seriously hurt, and I'm not just talking about physically, emotionally too." Josh's tone lowered as if he didn't want anyone else to overhear what he would say next. "Look, you know as much as I do what I would give for you to uncover some kind of information on your mom. Something that could give us closure after all this time."

Tara tried not to get upset with her dad. She knew deep down that he had the same suspicions that she did. But he needed to tell himself that she was gone to justify the life he had built since Tara's mom went missing in action. "Well then, forget I even brought it up." Tara had to stop talking before her voice began to crack. "I have to get going. There is someone else waiting for the satellite phone." Tara was completely lying, there was no one else in the tent with her, but she couldn't muster up anything else to say to her dad right now. "I love you, dad. I miss you so much. If you talk to Alicia, tell her I love and miss her too."

"Will do, Tara bug. And I will tell Dina that you send your love to her as well." Tara rolled her eyes and shook her head. "Oh yeah, tell Dina I said hello." And with that, Tara ended the call.

She honestly could care less about Dina, but for whatever reason, she made her dad happy.

She left the tent and decided to walk around the perimeter of what had been coined 'medical village.' Even though this area had been deemed safe, they were still living within chain-link and barb wire fencing. She walked along the fence line, staring up at the night sky. She had to admit, the constellations at night in Iraq were breathtaking. She stopped and inhaled deeply. Was her mom out there looking at the same stars?

Chapter Seven

EMILY

I must have blacked out. I wake up, and the heat that was burning at my legs seems to be gone. Then again, I'm not sure if I can feel my legs. I try to move my head but realize that I am upside down. I try to turn to my right, but a searing pain stabs me above my right eye. I try to breathe deep and swallow but realize I have no saliva to coat my throat. I breathe deep again and try not to let the dread that is creeping up take over. I can't see much of the Humvee, but what I can see is a total mess. There are brass casings everywhere from Simmons' M-249. The radio seems to be intact, but I have no idea where the handset is or working. I feel my breathing begin to pick up.

"Sanders, keep your shit together," I whisper to myself. This is not the time to lose my shit. It seems too quiet around me, but that could be just as dangerous as it could be safe. I whisper again, hoping that maybe one of the guys is in a similar position in the Humvee as I am. "Rodriguez? Simmons? Grant? You guys there?" I wait, hoping that if they are trapped, they can hear me. "Seriously, guys, I know I drive you crazy, but this is not time for the silent treatment. If you can hear me, make a noise, so I know you are there."

I wait, and I wait. Nothing. All I hear is the wind outside our Humvee. "Okay, Sanders, get your shit together and get the fuck up." It dawns on me that there could be a chance that either all the guys are unconscious and in worse shape than me, or they may be outside the truck somewhere and need my help. My right arm can move, and I decide to see if I can open the door. I feel around for the handle, trying to get my bearings on *where it is since I am upside down. They don't teach this shit in training, and who knows if it would even help right now. The pain above my eye spreads down the entire right side of my neck and into my shoulder. I keep moving my fingers over the door, but I can't find a grip on anything. "Dammit, Sanders! Find the goddamn handle!" I am now officially yelling at myself like our drill instructors used to do in basic training. I try to lean into my right shoulder, and the pain that I thought couldn't get any worse goes up to level 500 on the pain scale. I try to muffle my screams, but I can't. But somehow, through the pain, I manage to find the door handle with my fingertips. I try to grasp it, but my fingers slip. "FUCK!!!!!" I'm panting and think that I would rather go through childbirth again than deal with the pain travelling through my entire upper body. If only I could feel my goddam legs! I try to put pressure on them, but nothing. It's as though there is nothing below my waist. I begin to panic again but tuck that shit away. There is no time right now to worry about what is going on in my southern region. I lean more into my right side and try to project my fingers to stretch on their own volition. I feel the handle again, but this time, I latch on and ignore the pain that is now radiating in every single pore of my right side. I grab onto the latch and pull down with all my might. "FUCKKKKKK!" I fall out of the Humvee, and if I thought the pain was at 500 before, it's now somewhere in the thousands. I inhale hot sand and am instantly blinded by the blazing sun.*

I try to roll over onto my back but realize my legs are still partially trapped inside the Humvee. I am twisted into a figure eight position and realize that I am going to have to pull my legs out. I try to lift my head and shoulders, but my Kevlar feels like it weighs about a ton. I unstrap my chin strap and try the upright routine again. This time, my head and shoulders come off the ground but not without a price. It doesn't even seem like the screams are coming from my mouth. I must be having an out-of-body experience because I know my mouth is open, but I can't even hear myself screaming any longer.

I inhale sharply and use my left arm to push me up. My left side seems to be in a better shape than my right side, so I use my left arm to keep me propped up. I take my right arm and swing it forward to grab my pant leg. I try to grab on to ACU's, but as I reach for a piece of fabric, I realize barely any material left. This is the first time I see my legs in full view; they are almost completely burned through the ACU material, and in some places, I can see right through to my tibia. "No going back now, Sanders, suck this shit up and grab your damn legs. You can't feel them anyway." Back with the internal drill instructor yelling at myself again. I grab on to what I can and use what strength I can muster to pull my torched legs towards me. The power of gravity pulls them out of the Humvee, and I fall back on the ground. I give myself a minute to lay there and get my breathing back under control. I make a mental checklist of everything I need to get done.

- *I need water, stat.*

- *I need to assess my injuries as best I can.*

- *I need to determine if I have any working comms.*

- *And I need to check to make sure my guys are alive.*

I feel like shit for putting them last, but I am no good to them if I don't figure out what the fuck is wrong with my legs, and I need to radio in for support. After going through this list a few times in my head, so I don't forget it, I push myself back up with my left arm. I roll over onto my stomach and determine the best way to be mobile is going to be with the good ole Army low crawl. I take the deepest breath I have taken so far, knowing what new pain this will bring to my right arm and shoulder. I lean into my left side and decide that as long as that side doesn't scream in pain, I'll use it as my crutch. I shimmy around in a low crawl, mostly on my left side, so I can be situated to see back into the Humvee. Like a dumbass, I had my canteen leaning against the comms unit before my entire world went to shit. I pull myself back into the Humvee, so I can see into the cab. Of course, everything is in disarray, but I see Simmons's fancy water bottle that his fiancé had recently sent him laying on its side not that far from me. I stretch as far as I can grab onto the handle of the bottle. It's about halfway full! God Bless!! I drag it towards me and sit up, leaning on the bar between the Humvee front and back seat. I try not to be greedy with the drinking, but I end up downing almost every drop in the bottle. I find some way to stop myself because who knows if I will find any more any time soon. I wipe my mouth with the back of my hand and close my eyes for a minute. I know when I open them again, it's time to go down my checklist.

Water- check. Now to move on to assessing my injuries. I begin at the top of my head, and lucky for me, find a shard of the side mirror on the ground not far from me. I find the root of the searing pain in my head. I have a giant gaping wound, it could be from my Kevlar helmet or shrapnel. Either way, it's pretty deep, at least a few inches deep. Before I jump the gun and use my only first aid kit on this wound, I decide to keep moving down my body. The rest of my face seems to be good if you disregard the hundreds of scratches and what looks like dirt, but I bet it has bits of shrapnel pockmarked all over my face. I move on to my arms.

I am pretty confident my right arm is dislocated and am so grateful that Grant, our medic, taught me how to reset a dislocated shoulder. I make a mental note to come back to that once I finish my assessment. I still have my flak vest on and do a quick scan over it. Seems like the core part of my body is all intact with no major issues. Thank goodness for small blessings, right? I keep moving down and get to the worst part of all. My legs. Both my thighs seem to be in decent shape, there seems to be some shrapnel poking out in areas, but again, I will deal with those if I have enough supplies to tend to them. It gets awful once I scan past my knee caps. Both of my lower legs are pretty much burnt to shit. My left boot looks like it is completely melted into my foot. My right tibia is shining white with burnt pieces of flesh curled up around the opening; this seems to be the worst of it. I lean back and stare up at the sky.

"Dammit, Grant, I really hope you are somewhere around here because I sure as shit could use your medical assistance right now," I say this to the sky as if Grant is some medical genie that will appear from behind a cloud. I realize I may be beginning to hallucinate as I think I hear footsteps coming. Considering we are in hostile territory and we were just blown up, I want to hope for the best. But then I hear the worst sound I can ask for. I hear men talking in Arabic. I want to cry; I want to crawl into a fucking ball and cry for my dad to rescue me. I forget all my training for a split second and am a five-year-old girl again that had a nightmare. This has to be a nightmare. I must wake up any second now.

The voices get closer and louder. I only know basic words and phrases in Arabic and only when they are spoken slowly. These guys mean business and are speaking at a rampant pace. I reach down and realize my side arm is still attached to my thigh holster. Again, thank God for small blessings. I reach down with my dislocated right arm and slowly unclip my 9mm from its holster. The voices get louder, and I raise my arm, propping it up with my left hand. I turn the safety off and figure if I'm going to die, I am going to kill as many pieces of shit as I can in the process.

The voices are on the other side of the Humvee. They stop at the rear left side and lower their voices. They see me. I know it. I can't understand them, but I know it. The footsteps slowly begin moving again, and I turn in their direction. I pull the trigger as the first insurgent comes around the rear corner of the Humvee. With my dislocated arm, I hit him in the knee cap, enough to take him down. Chaos breaks out. I keep shooting, but then everything goes black again.

I am so thankful that he has been away on business for longer than usual. Yes, this means that our meals are simple meals consisting of only rice and what vegetables we are able to grow, but I would eat this way forever if it meant never having that monster come back. I daydream that perhaps he dies somehow on one of his trips. But then I think about the children and me. I have no idea what would happen to us if he wasn't able to provide for us, and I hate him even more. But not nearly as much as I hate myself for succumbing to this life. If only I could have been stronger to keep fighting, I could have gotten him to kill me. Why didn't I fight more?

I pull the crystal out from the folds of my clothing and squeeze it as if it truly will heal me. I don't believe in such things, but the children do. They have told me that it seems as though I am walking better, and they do not hear me crying in my sleep at night. Little do they know that it has less to do with the crystal and everything to do with the monster not being here.

But just like everything else in my life, all good things must come to an end. Asad and I are sitting in the shade in front of our hut while Khayru and Lulu practice their English alphabet in the dirt. I hear his voice before I see him. I take a deep breath and pull at my hijab to cover most of my face. I look down at Asad and squeeze him a little closer to me. Perhaps the monster will not notice me and keep walking. I keep my eyes down and notice not just his feet but Maimun and Mahir's sandaled feet too. I breathe a sigh of relief because I hope this means he will just keep walking into the hut. Normally, a runner would have brought me some sort of meat to prepare for his return, so seeing him with our sons is quite the shock.

I keep looking down at Asad's dirty little hands in my lap. The footsteps stop a few feet away from me. "Woman, the older boys will be taking the younger children back to the medical village tomorrow. It has been asked why you have not received your shots since you still have more birth-giving years left in you." Mohammad has picked up his English from the older boys, and for once, I hate myself for ever teaching them my language. "Due to your good behavior lately, I have instructed Maimun and Mahir to take you with them." My heart skips a beat. Did he just say that I will be leaving our hut? I try to mask my excitement and keep my eyes down. I did not miss the part he said about my child bearing years. So, he will be planning on raping me again soon for another baby. I almost wish I had not been under such good behavior to deserve this trip.

"Did you hear anything I just said to you, woman?" Now he crouches down and takes his hand to pull my chin up. I have no choice but to look him square in his monstrous black eyes. I want to vomit just looking at him, but I choke it down. I do not say a word, but I nod my head that I understand. I know this is a trick to see if I will speak. If I did open my mouth to reply, it would have been smacked shut with the back of his hand.

"Mahir, when Malika arrives home from school, have her take the woman to Shabir's hut for a bath. She is beyond filthy." And with this, Mohammad stands back up and walks away from the hut.

I have so many mixed emotions running through my body. I will not only have the chance to interact with other people, but I will receive a bath. In the 15 years or more that I have been a prisoner here, I have never been bathed. Yes, I have been given wet rags to clean off my body, but I had not cleansed my entire body since before my world went to hell. I look up at the boys that are trying to hide their excitement for me.

"How did you make this happen, Mahir? How can this even be possible?" I am trying to control my emotions, but for the second time recently, these children have become my saviors, and they have no clue what this means for me. Mahir looks at Maimun and then back down at me. "Well, we can't take all the credit for it. One of the doctors at the medical village asked me about our mother and younger siblings. She was the one that mentioned that if you are still having children, it is important for you to be vaccinated too." Mahir shrugs, and my heart sinks a bit. So, this wasn't 100% his idea, but a curious doctor. This could still be helpful to me. My hopeful thoughts come back to me, and I think about all the possibilities of how I could send a message of some sort out to the world.

"Well, thank you, boys, for convincing your father to allow me to go. I know that must not have been an easy task." I smile at them both, and they nod their heads and proceed into the hut.

I gather up Asad and the other children to begin preparing dinner. I assume since the monster walked away, perhaps he will not be back for our humble supper tonight. The rest of the day goes by in a fog to me. I am reminded of my early days after I had earned the right to be out of my hole for a few hours at a time. I felt the same way as if everything around me was enveloped in a fog; as if I am in a dream state, and at any moment, I will wake up and be home with Josh and our sweet little girls.

After eating our rice for supper, Malika helps me down the dirt road away from our hut. How many times early on did I attempt to run away down this same road? Only to be captured every time by one of the monster's men. They would drag me back to the hut, with kickings and screamings. Once I had taught myself to walk again after my legs had healed, all I wanted to do was run away. I had no idea where I would go or if I would even find any friendly forces, but I persisted. Time and time again.

So now, to be walking with my oldest daughter to take a bath was almost surreal. I struggle to keep up with her young and fresh legs. Although my legs healed up years ago, the damage sustained was permanent. I walk with a terrible limp, practically dragging my right leg behind me. The older boys made me a cane from an old tree limb years ago, and that has been a godsend to help me around.

Malika is quiet and stares straight ahead. If I had to guess, she is concerned with what this means. Since she is the oldest daughter, she pays attention to how her father treats me. Nothing gets by Malika. I can see in her a fire to speak up and fight back, but she is wise too. She has seen the results of fighting back and not just with her father. I know the older men in the village similarly treat their women the same way. For the first time, it occurs to me- what if there are other women like me in our village? What if I am not the only female soldier they captured, tortured, and raped repeatedly over the years? In all my suffering and survival, it never once had occurred to me that there could be more women in the same situation that I was in; an imprisoned human baby factory taken captive to keep creating more monsters for their miserable insurgent army.

Malika stops abruptly and looks at me. "Mama, you must promise me you will not try to run away once you are in Shabir's hut? I must have your word on this." Her stare is so fierce, so strong. I hope one day she makes it out of this god-forsaken hell hole. "Malika," I take her hand with my free left hand, "even if I wanted to run, how could I? I can barely walk the short distance we covered to get here." I squeeze her hand and smile at her.

She smiles back and squeezes my hand, "I think you have more fight in you than you let us on to believe, but I need reassurance. I can't take watching him hurt you again. I know he is my father, but you are my mama. I will not sit back any longer and allow him to treat you in such a cruel way." I sigh and let go of her hand. "Nothing gets by you, Malika. You are wise beyond your years. But now you must promise me that you will never, and I mean never, intervene when your father is dealing with me. My fight is not your fight or burden to bear."

And with that, our conversation is over. We walk up the path to Shabir's hut, and I notice that it is similar to our own, but they have electricity inside. There is one single light bulb dangling from the mud-packed ceiling, and I am in awe. I have not had electricity or running water in so long; such a small luxury I always took for granted until they were both gone.

Shabir meets us at her doorway and greets Malika in Arabic. Shabir looks at me quickly but then turns her head and signals us to follow her inside. We walk into the main room, where the lonely light bulb dangles from the ceiling glowing like the small first-world miracle that it is to me. Shabir and her family must be wealthier or more prominent in the village because her hut is larger, with several smaller rooms off of the main room. She leads us into what I would gather as close as possible in this village to a bathroom. There is a cast iron tub in the center of the room, and it is filled a little more than halfway with murky but what appears to be clean water. Shabir speaks to Malika again, I assume instructing her on what to do with me. Clearly, I will need help even getting into the tub. I have not had a reason to lift my legs up and over anything in so long. I am not confident I even have the range of motion required to make this happen. Malika replies to Shabir, and they bow their heads to each other. With that, Shabir looks at me again very quickly and puts a sheet of fabric up to cover the doorway.

Malika looks at me and smiles timidly. "Um, I have to stay in here with you. Shabir said that you might need my help getting into the tub and out when you are finished."

I can tell this is very awkward for Malika, she has never seen me naked before, and modesty is taken very seriously in their culture. I reach out and grab her hand again and squeeze, "Thank you, Malika. I know this is not easy for you, and I promise it's not any easier for me. But yes, Shabir is right, I fear I will need help getting in and out." And with that, I set to taking off my makeshift dress, which are just oversized rags stitched together. Honestly, I can't even remember the last time I saw myself naked, and who knows what condition some of my scars were even in. As I drop the rags from my shoulders and remove my hijab, I hear Malika gasp.

Ah yes, my legs. None of the children has ever seen the condition of my legs before. Since I was captured when the wounds were fresh, my shins and feet became severely infected during the months I was trapped in a hole in the ground. Somehow, they both had healed, but there were not pretty to look at. My right leg was the worse. My last two toes were gone, and my ankle permanently was swollen and forced my foot to turn inwards more than it naturally should. From the ankle up, the skin looked more like a lizard or snake's skin than a human. It was shiny like scales and raised skin. In the middle of my shin, there was a gaping hole. All the muscle and tendons had been burned away, and when it was fresh, I could see right to the bone. Luckily, the skin had naturally grown over the bone, but nothing was left to protect the bone beneath the scaly skin.

"Mama, wh, wh," Malika stuttered, something she hadn't done since she was a little thing learning how to speak in English. "What happened to you?" The tears in her eyes begin to well up, and I literally can't handle one more second of her pity. "Another life, Malika. Another life. Now, why don't we get this over with? You have no idea how long I have wanted a bath." I muster up the strength to lift my right leg first. My left side has always remained my strongest, so I decide to use that as leverage to hurl my right leg up over the brim of the tub. Malika holds on to my right elbow, and I grab the rim with my left arm and hoist myself into the tub. My right leg follows the mental commands I was secretly giving it, and I take a deep breath. "That wasn't as bad as I thought it would be," I smile weakly at Malika, hoping to get her to stop the stream of tears that are now openly streaming down her cheeks. "Please, Malika, you must not say anything to your brothers about my legs, okay? Like I said, it was another life." Malika nods, and I finish getting my body into the lukewarm water. I slowly sit down, reveling in every single moment. I have no idea when another chance will come about for me, and I have learned to cherish them as they come.

Malika hands me a bar of white soap and a rag to clean up with. I hold the bar to my nose and inhale. It smells so clean! I begin to wash away the dirt on my skin. The dirt is so caked on in areas that I look darker than some of my children. I begin to scrub frantically, wanting to shed every piece of dirt, sand, and filth from him off me. I begin scrubbing so hard; I don't even notice that I am sobbing. I look up, and Malika is crouched down in the corner with her head in her hands. She, too, is sobbing, and without me having to explain anything, I think she has begun to figure out my story.

Once I have finished washing my entire body, I unbraid my hair. Again, it has been so long since my hair was clean, that one would not even know that the natural color is an ashy blonde color. I lean my head back to allow all my hair to soak in the water. I was not offered any shampoo, and I don't ask. I plan on using the bar of soap on my hair as well. I lather up the soap and work through sections of my hair. It's almost to my knees when it's not braided, and it takes a while. Malika notices me struggling with getting the soap out of my hair and comes over to help me. "Mama, your hair is golden like the sun?" She says this as a question which makes me realize again that she is lining up all these clues in her mind to solve later. In all the years of giving birth and raising these children, none of them has ever seen me without my head wrapped. Even if they had seen my hair, it was so matted and dirty, not just with sand, but there was still dried blood on my scalp from the initial explosion. There would have been no way for them to know my hair was blonde.

I don't know how to reply, so I stick with the same response I have given her so far, "From another life, Malika. Let's just leave it at that, okay?" She clears her throat and helps me finish my hair. She then helps me out of the tub, which seems to be a little more difficult than getting in. My hips became stiff from sitting in the tub for so long, but I would do it all over again if it meant I could be clean.

Once I am out of the tub and dry off, Malika helps me into a new set of clothing. I guess he does not want me to be seen in public in my normal rags. This must be my version of rags to riches. I wish I could laugh at this thought, but I know all of this will come with a price. Before the end of the month, I am certain he will rape me, and I will be pregnant again.

After I am dressed, Malika braids my hair for me, which is a wonderful reprieve; the bath, the act of cleansing, all of it has drained me. I am utterly exhausted and have no clue how I will make the walk back to our little hut. When Malika is finished, she places a hand on each of my shoulders and rests her chin softly on the top of my head. "Mama, you keep saying that all these scars are from another life, but I do not understand. I am old enough for you to tell me. I want to know what happened to you. Did papa do this to you?" I take a deep breath, knowing that she truly could never know the truth of what happened to me. It would make her too much of a liability, and I remind myself that it is not her fault she was born into this nightmare.

I reach up and pat her hands on my shoulders. "Sweet Malika, just know that everything that has happened to me has made me stronger. One day you will understand why I am this way, and I pray that it will not change your views of the world." And with that, we gather my dirty rags and begin the trek back to our hut.

Chapter Eight

TARA

~

"Tara! Earth to Tara!" Nick taunted Tara as he threw small pieces from his protein bar in Tara's direction. They were sitting in the shade behind the Medical Village. The summer heat had begun to subside, but not by much. They were approaching September, and it still proved to bring on some pretty intense afternoons. "Sorry, Nick. I guess I zoned out for a minute." Tara tried to give Nick a smile, but she knew he could see right through her. She had been trying to keep her suspicions and thoughts to herself about her mom, but she needed to tell him now before taking action into her own hands to determine if what she thought was true.

"Nick, I need to bounce some ideas off you, and I need you to keep an open mind about it." She stood up and began to pace as this seemed to be the only way she was able to communicate recently.

"Okay, I'm listening." Nick put down his half-eaten protein bar and sat up a little straighter, following her as she paced back and forth. "You know those two young men that are helping us from the village nearby?" Nick nodded, and Tara continued, "Well, I may have cornered Doc into giving them jobs because I think they may know something about my mom." Tara stopped pacing and looked down at Nick.

"Um, okay, you do realize these boys were not even alive when your mom went missing? Like, what could they possibly know?" Nick stood up, brushing the sand off the back of his khakis. He walked right in front of Tara and pulled her chin up, so she was looking right at him. "Look, I told you I would support you and help you find answers about your mom, but harassing two boys may not be the right way to go about this. Maybe it's time to talk to Doc about this. Maybe he has some contacts here that could help." Tara pulled away from Nick, knowing fully well if she kept staring into his eyes, he would enthrall her into agreeing with him.

"Nick, you know I can't do that. I know it seems peaceful here, but I have heard bits and pieces of conversations among locals in lines throughout each day. There are people who live here that still do not trust us. I can't put Doc or anyone else here in danger." Tara began to pace again. "So convincing Doc to hire them wasn't the only thing I may have done. I may have planted a seed with the boys to allow me to come to their village to give their mom her vaccinations." Tara took a deep breath and stopped pacing again.

Nick crossed his arms over his chest and sighed. "Tara, I love you with my whole heart and soul. You know this." Tara knew a 'but' was coming, so she beat him to the punch. "Let me guess, Nick, but you just can't watch me self-destruct and make stupid decisions like this? You know, when you asked me to marry you, you knew what you were getting. I have been spending my entire life since my mom went missing planning for how I would find her. It's hard enough watching my dad, my entire family, and the goddam Army give up on her, but I refuse to do the same!" And with that, Tara knew this conversation would have no positive ending for the night. She turned around to storm off, only to see Rosie walking towards them. From the look on Rosie's face, it was pretty clear that she more than likely overheard more than Tara wanted her to hear. Tara walked right past Rosie, bee lining it for the female tent.

"Tara, wait up!" Rosie was jogging to catch up to her. Tara stopped, knowing that Nick was probably still standing where she had left him, but her anger had drained all her energy from her, and she truly didn't want to fight with Nick. Tara turned around to face Rosie. "Hey Chica, is everything okay? I don't mean to pry, but I couldn't help but overhear your conversation with Nick." Rosie always had a way of getting straight to the point, and normally, this was one of the traits that Tara loved about Rosie. Right now, it was not something Tara appreciated. "Rosie, I don't want to talk about it. It's just too much to get into right here." Tara looked back and saw Nick walking towards them.

Rosie grabbed Tara by the hand and began to pull her towards the path to the female tents. "Well, it's a good thing that I got my hands on some local hooch. Let's go back to our tent, and you can start from the very beginning." Tara wanted to question Rosie on where she had gotten her hands on some alcohol, but she knew Rosie would see right through that as stalling. Rosie looked back at Nick and waved at him. 'It's all good, Nick; I can take it from here." Rosie gave him a casual military salute, and Nick just nodded and took off towards where the male tents were stationed. Once Tara and Rosie were in Rosie's corner of the female tent, Rosie closed them in with her makeshift blanket curtain. She then took a brown bottle out of her trunk, grabbed two plastic bottles that are typically used for urine samples, and poured the clear liquid into each cup. "Rosie, please tell me those are new cups and not used ones." Tara was half-joking, but considering the bottle's condition, she was genuinely concerned with Rosie's judgement making calls at the moment. "Please, Chica, give me a little bit of credit. Of course, they are brand new. Even if they weren't, the potency of what's in this bottle would easily kill any lingering germs." Rosie smiled her sly grin and handed Tara a glass. "Cheers, Tara. I have a feeling your story is going to need more of this, so let's get to it."

With that, Tara tipped her plastic cup full of potent clear liquor to Rosie's cup, and she slammed back her first shot. Before she knew it, she was starting from the beginning, just like Rosie had told her to do. Talking about what she could remember about her mom, most of it just stories that her dad had told her so many times that Tara had stored them away in her memory as if she had been old enough to remember. She talked about growing up as an Army brat and seeing her mom walk away from her for the last time. Tara was too young to understand the severity of war back then. Her mom and dad had always told her their jobs were to keep the monsters out of her and her sister's bedroom at night. Little did she know then what that would cost her family. She recalled her dad sitting her down and telling her that mommy was a little lost but that the Army was doing everything they could to find her. She pushed back on her dad, even at such a young age, "But Daddy, Mommy is so good at directions. She would never get lost in the dessert." Again, it wasn't until much later in Tara's life would she learn the whole truth behind what had happened to her mom.

Tara went on to talk about how she always felt deep in her soul that her mom was still alive. She shared how weird it was to bury an empty coffin and how everyone kept telling her how brave her mom was and a true American Hero. One of the soldiers that had been in the vehicle with Tara's mom kept in contact with her and her dad over the years. Rodriguez was almost like an uncle to her. When Tara was a senior in high school, she went and stayed with him and his wife for a week in the summer. That is when Roddie, as her mom had always called him, told her how guilty he felt all these years later. He, too, was not sold on the Army's declaration that her mom was dead. He vividly remembered pulling on her arm, and he thought he could feel a pulse, but they were being attacked from all sides and had incurred so many losses. They had no choice but to leave Emily and their medic, Grant, behind.

As Tara shared all this with Rosie, Rosie remained quiet, rubbing Tara's back when the words became too hard to share, and her tears took over. Tara finally explained that everything she had done since pretty much middle school had been to get her to Iraq. This was her lifelong mission, and now she was here and felt just as helpless as she did when she was a little girl looking at an empty coffin being lowered into the ground.

When Tara was finished, Rosie wrapped her arms around Tara and brought her in for a long hug.

"Chica, I had no idea you had been through so much. You are the strongest woman I know." Rosie pulled back and looked straight into Tara's eyes, "You know I'm not playing when I say that, right?" Tara chuckled at Rosie's straight shooter mentality once again. "Yes, Rosie, I know you are serious. And thank you. Other than Nick, you are the only other friend I have ever told the entire story to from start to finish." Tara did feel a weight lifted off her shoulders. She knew she could trust Rosie and hopefully could rely on her for support if it came to that. "Girl, I am your ride or die. If you believe, no, if you feel it in your gut that your mama is alive, then I will do whatever you need me to do to help find her." And with that, Rosie filled up their cups with the last of the hooch left in the brown glass bottle.

Chapter Nine

EMILY

~

I remember getting the girls ready that morning; my girl, that is my sweet baby Alicia, with her dimpled chubby cheeks. She was just a baby. How could any good mom leave her sweet baby girl like this? But I had to go. My unit's numbers were up, and we needed to go. Josh had already been to Afghanistan right after 9/11. He reassured me that my unit's mission would be safe; we shouldn't even need to leave the wire for any reason. I still felt guilty; Tara was only four and hadn't even started pre-school yet. Alicia wasn't even walking, and here I was, leaving them both behind with their Special Forces dad and grandparents to raise them. I added Alicia's bow to her hair, just like her big sister's. We tried to explain to Tara where Mommy was going. We told her that Mommy had to fight the monsters just like her Daddy had done when she was a little older than Alicia. She would nod her head and tell me that she wasn't afraid of the monsters. God, I wish I was as brave as she was.

As quickly as this memory came into my brain, it was gone. Drifting through like the fog we were beginning to see in the early mornings, being so close to the mountains. I finish getting Asad and Khayru dressed in their handmade gowns from their older brothers. I did my best to keep what clothes I had for the children clean and in decent condition. I was not given much to take care of them, and it wasn't their fault they were brought into this world by a monster.

Malika walks in with Lulu, "Mama, the boys are ready to go." I nod my head and give a weak smile to Asad and Khayru. "Alright then, let's get moving." I was nervous about the walk. We were leaving quite early because I had warned Mahir that I would need to take several breaks and would probably need to walk at the pace of a snail. This led to a lengthy explanation to the younger children, who had no idea what a snail was. Mahir said that he was able to borrow a donkey from one of the elders for me and baby Asad to ride on. This still made me worry, as I was not even sure I would be strong enough to sit on the back of a donkey.

With the help of Mahir and Maimun, I was able to get on the donkey and kept my legs to one side. Malika placed Asad in my arms, and I swaddled him close to me so he would not fidget and try to jump out. He was closely approaching his 2nd birthday and was getting more active by the minute; Malika gently squeezed the top of my knee and gave me a secret smile of encouragement. She had been quiet since the bath experience the night before. I hope she keeps her promise to me not to share with her older brothers what she saw and what we had talked about. Although those boys seemed to love me and care for me, I know their monster of a father held a close bond with them, and I am sure if it came down to it, they would always side with him.

We began to move, with Mahir and Maimun leading the donkey. Lulu was old enough to walk, and she held Malika's hand while Khayru was hanging on to Malika's neck with his legs wrapped around her waist. He looked back at me and smiled. It dawned on me that this was also their first true encounter outside of our little hut world for the youngest three. Lulu had begun to walk to the well in the village for water, but the youngest two boys were always with me. If Khayru only knew how excited I was as well. I tried to contain my excitement to myself the evening before. Mohammad never returned, but I didn't want to alert the children as to why I would ever be so excited to see a doctor. I still didn't have a plan as to how I could try to signal to anyone at the medical village who I was or that I needed help. All I can do is hope that the right person will help us, and I will signal them somehow, but then the doubts begin to overtake me again. This had been the inner battle I had fought with myself throughout the night too. Even if I was able to get a message across somehow, what next? After all these years, I had no clue indeed where we lived. I barely remembered the location of the ambush. For years, I tried to keep the last grid coordinates on repeat in my mind, but those numbers fleeted my memory over time.

As we made the trek to the medical village, I paid attention to every single detail along the way. Every mud hut we passed, every barren tree and the random food stands set up along the route. I tried not to stare at the people we passed for fear of being caught looking at men, but I memorized all their faces as much as I could. If I could find a way to be alone with a doctor or medic, then I could describe to them the way back to where I lived. Yes. This is how I would get out of this hell hole. Oh, but the children? What would become of them? Would he take out his aggression on them if I was gone? I prayed he would not turn Malika into his new baby factory. The thoughts and fears kept nagging at me as we continued on our way.

Finally, after several hours of walking and stopping for Lulu, I could see up in the distance of a group of tents. I tried not to let the tears pool in my eyes, but it was inevitable. It reminded me so much of a military camp, which made me wonder if it was one after all. When the children kept saying medical village, I was thinking it would be huts like we lived in. I had no idea it would be the standard-issue military tents surrounded by fencing and concertina wire. My heartbeat picked up as we got closer. I actually may have a solid chance at getting out of here. If this was still a military base, then they would take me immediately!

But as we got closer, there were no Army or Marines on guard duty. In fact, I couldn't see any uniformed military personnel anywhere. Everyone inside the camp were in civilian clothing. My heart sank. So, this was a medical village, probably just using what military equipment had been left over after the main portion of the war was done. Even though I had gotten my hopes up a few minutes before, I was still going to try to send some sort of message out to someone. Anyone. I had to try.

Chapter Ten

TARA

"Good morning, sunshine!" Rosie was pulling back Tara's sleeping bag in a way too perky manner, considering how much hooch they had drunk the night before. "Ugh, Rosie! What the hell are you doing? My alarm didn't even go off yet. Let me sleep!" Tara tried to pull back the top of her sleeping bag, but Rosie was more awake and was in a better state to hold the covers back from Tara.

"Well, Chica, since you passed out before setting your alarm last night, I took the liberty of giving you an early morning wake-up. Plus, you know all the good eggs are gone by the time you usually make it over to the mess tent." Rosie sat there, waiting for Tara to make a move to get up. Tara slowly sat up, rubbing her temples as the all-too-common hangover began to set in. "How in God's green earth are you even alive right now? And at that, how are you so cheerful? I feel like death warmed over." Rosie hands Tara some ibuprofen and a bottle of water without even skipping a beat. "I got you covered, Chica. Take these and then get dressed. I am pretty certain there may be a dreamy tall guy with the best man bun around waiting for your outside our tent."

Nick. Tara thought back to how her night had started and how she had walked away from him upset. And then she proceeded to drink way too much hooch and, oh yeah, tell her entire life story to Rosie. Sometimes, she really regretted her actions, and although this was nowhere near as bad as spring break of 2016, this still ranked up there. She had never told anyone other than Nick her story. She was always worried that people would feel sorry for her, and then if they knew her life plans and goals, they would think she was bat shit crazy, but she trusted Rosie on a deeper level, plus what did she have to lose with Rosie knowing? If anything, she now had a solid advocate, even if Nick didn't believe her or want to support her any longer. "I probably owe him an apology or something," Tara said as she downed her hangover cure. "Well, I know it's at least the something part." Rosie winked at Tara and stood up over her cot. "Okay then, you get dressed, and I will see you and your dreamy man bun guy at breakfast." Tara smiled and waved her friend goodbye so she could get dressed.

After taking a quick shower and brushing away her terrible hooch breath, Tara was ready to face Nick. As Rosie promised, he was waiting outside the front of the female tent. "Hey there, handsome," Tara said as Nick opened up his arms for her to walk into. Nick gave the best hugs, and Tara didn't realize how badly she needed one until she was well within his reach. "I am so sorry for being such a jerk to you last night," Tara said as she snuggled in even closer to his chest.

Nick squeezed her tight and rested his chin on the top of her head. "Don't even sweat it, kid. You know I love you with my whole heart and soul. I should be the one apologizing. I know what I signed up for when I asked you to be my wife." At this, Tara pulled away just enough so she could look up into his eyes. She loved this man so much. He had been her rock all through undergrad. Why she even thought to question his loyalty to her or her beliefs about her mother was ridiculous. She knew he would support her no matter what. "I love you too, Nicholas Lombardo. I can't way to be Mrs. Tara Lombardo one day." And with that, Nick leaned down and brought Tara in for a sweet, loving kiss.

"Okay, you two lovebirds, let's get some breakfast!" Rosie came jogging around the corner and smacked Tara on the butt. "Rosita Montoya, I swear you have the timing of a sewer rat!" Nick said jokingly as they all began to walk towards the mess tent. Tara walked between the two of them, holding Nick's hand and feeling so grateful to have both him and Rosie in her life. She now had not one but two rocks in her life, and with them both standing by her side, she had a renewed confidence that she would find out what happened to her mom.

After breakfast was over, Tara and Nick stole one more kiss before going their separate ways for the day. Tara and Rosie grabbed their gear and headed to their respective medical tents. "Tara," Rosie stopped walking, forcing Tara to stop too. "I want you to know that I meant what I said last night. I will support you however I can with your mom. Why don't we talk some more tonight and make a plan, but this time we will be sober." She gave Tara that sly smile, and Tara smiled back. "I would love that, Rosie. I have some ideas, but I think talking them out and weighing our options is the best way to go about this." "Sounds like a plan, Chica!" Rosie smiled an even bigger smile and headed off to her work area. Tara's headache had begun to go away, her fiancé wasn't mad at her, and her closest co-worker was proving to become her best friend. The day hadn't even started yet, but Tara was feeling great about the day.

She headed off to her medical tent and began setting up her work station for the day when she saw Doc heading her way. "Good morning Doc!" Tara greeted him enthusiastically. "Well, good morning to you too, Sanders! You seem to be in a good mood, and hopefully, my news will make your day even better." Tara stopped setting up her medical supplies and stood up straighter to listen to Doc. "Okay, you now have my undivided attention." Doc leaned against the tent pole and began looking at the clipboard he was always keeping with him. "Remember a while back you mentioned you would be willing to travel to some of the farther villages to reach families that couldn't make the trek?" Tara's pulse picked up at what Doc was about to tell her. "Yes, of course, I remember that, and I am still interested! When do we leave?" Tara bent down and began to pack her supplies back up in her medical bag.

"Ha-ha, I had a feeling you would say that. We need to be ready to leave within the hour. It's going to be you, me, your lovebird Nick and a few others." Doc was already beginning to walk away; Tara assumed to finish notifying the others. Without any hesitation, she grabbed her medical bag and jogged back to her tent to pack a personal bag.

By the time she finished, she barely had time to stop by Rosie's work station and let her know what was going on. Tara met the rest of their small group by the 'office' tent, as they all called it. Doc took attendance, and they all loaded up into the jeep. Tara had no clue if the smaller village they would be visiting had any connection to her mom, but this was a start. For the last few months, she had been stewing on the idea that her mom was somehow connected to Mahir and his family, but she knew Nick was right.

She needed to explore other outlets too. She couldn't become 100% fixated on this one hunch.

As they drove away, Tara could already see the groups of families making their way to the medical village. She felt guilty leaving Rosie and the rest of the team short-staffed because it looked like it would be a busy day, especially as she saw several larger families already coming through the gates.

It took Doc and the team close to six hours to make their way to their first stop. They would spend the afternoon in this village, share a meal with the locals, and sleep outside the jeep. Tara was a little nervous about being exposed like this, but so far, their time in Iraq had been peaceful. Combat operations had been over for several years, and Doc would not risk their lives if he did not feel 100% safe himself. Once the team unloaded all their equipment, Doc went to meet with the local elders to discuss the best way to treat the villagers. They decided it would be best to move the jeep under one shady tree at the center of the village near the well. From there, the team of medics opened up the back of the jeep and made a small patient area there. They had brought several cots, so they set those up for patients to sit on while waiting to be seen. Within a short time, the locals began popping out of their huts, having stayed hidden at first since they were not used to seeing Americans since the war had ended, according to Doc. Many of the children were not used to seeing Americans in a peaceful manner, so they were beyond timid at first. Tara's heart began to quicken as she saw several entire families approaching with women in tow. She tried to remain focused on her work, but she kept scanning the women to see if she could catch a glimpse of green eyes or paler skin.

As the day progressed, Tara was so busy not only giving immunizations out and recording medical history but also with several well-child physicals. There were many children that would need after care, so she made a mental note to talk to Doc about a return trip here in a few months. Due to her being so busy, Tara had lost focus on looking out for anyone that may look like her mother. She tried to engage some families in conversation, but even though her Arabic was fluent, many locals would barely even look at her, let alone have any sort of conversation with her.

At the end of the workday, Tara and the rest of the team packed up the jeep exhausted. Doc instructed them to wash up with water from the well and meet him by the elder's hut. They would have dinner with the elder and his family, which was considered a huge honor to villagers. As Tara and Nick walked over to the hut, Tara nudged Nick in the side, "So, you up for this meal?" She asked him teasingly, knowing how picky of an eater he was. Lucky for him, most of the food back at camp was standard American food. But he had struggled the week they were in Kuwait. So, she knew this was going to be a fun dinner. Nick nudged her back and smiled, "Considering how serious that elder looks? I don't think I get a say on if I eat or not. I am not trying to piss that dude off!" Tara and Nick laughed and made their way over to Doc and the others.

By the time dinner was over, Tara couldn't believe how tired she was. She didn't even care if she had to sleep on the hard ground. There were only two cots, and they had done the most professional process for determining who should sleep on them-Rock, Paper, Scissors. She lost, which wasn't all that bad since Nick lost too. Since they had been in Iraq, they were not allowed to sleep in the same tent, even though they were engaged. As they rolled out their sleeping bags on the ground, she thought about how just last night she had been a total jerk to him. Even though she had apologized, she still felt terrible about it. She promised herself if they were going to have a future together, she had to get her anger under control because Nick deserved better than that.

Nick laid his sleeping bag next to Tara's, and he nudged her as she was getting her makeshift bed. "This is the first time in months I get to wake up next to you." Nick winks at Tara, and her heart melts. "I know I already apologized, Nick, but I just need to say it again. I'm sorry I doubted you last night and stormed off like that. I don't know how I got so lucky to be your future wife." Tara grabbed Nick's hand and gave it a good squeeze. She wanted to reach up and give him a big kiss, but she didn't dare do that in the middle of the village. Tara laid down that night, exhausted but with peace in her heart.

Chapter Eleven

EMILY

The first time he raped me, I laid there in the dirt, praying I would die; praying that my injuries, my infected leg, or something, anything, would kill me. He had turned me onto my stomach, and my face had been pressed against the dirt floor of my cell. He kept one hand on the base of my skull, which was still bruised and sore from being pistol-whipped after he had found me next to the Humvee. I was already naked, having had my uniform stripped away from me when I had been unconscious. It was nothing but a quick task for him to take care of his clothes and begin the deed. I tried to float away, but between the pain in my skull and the pain between my legs, I wept. I wept into the sand and dirt for the life I had. I wept for my children I now knew I would never see again. I wept for Josh, my wonderful and amazing husband, who would never in a million years treat me like this because he wasn't a monster like this man. He got up and left as quickly as he had come down the ladder without saying a word. If I didn't die from my injuries, I would die fighting to get out of here.

Once we entered the medical village, Mahir led us over to a tent that appeared to be some sort of administration tent. Mahir began speaking to a woman, probably in her fifties, and it appeared that she might be in charge. Mahir and the woman began walking over to our group. I could tell that this woman knew Mahir in a work-related fashion, and it occurred to me that Mahir worked here. How amazing to see him in a different light. Here, Mahir and Maimun were not her sons but employees. They were translators, and it was apparent that they were held in high esteem. The woman stopped in front of the donkey, and Mahir cleared his throat to get my attention.

"Mama, this is Nurse Sue. She is Doc's wife and takes care of all the paperwork for the medical village, as well as paying Maimun and me." Nurse Sue smiles at me and sticks out her hand to shake mine.

"It is so nice to finally meet you, Ma'am. You have raised two wonderful young men. You should be very proud of them." I have not had human interaction like this in so long; I just look down and stare at the ground. I do not shake her hand for fear of not being able to let go, or worse yet, I may begin to cry.

The kind nurse takes her hand back and looks at Mahir. "Well, Mahir, why don't we get your mother and siblings a snack, and then we can get down to business."

Mahir leads the group over to a small cluster of trees, and Maimun helps me off the donkey. Malika takes Asad from me, and we make our way over to a canopy tent with tables and chairs set up underneath it. The kind nurse sweeps her arm out for us to sit down. Mahir and Maimun, having worked here for a while now, disappear behind the tents and reappear with granola bars, fruit snacks, and bottled water. If I thought I would cry before, just from an American speaking to me, I was on the verge of tears now. I hadn't seen food in any sort of packaging for so long. My mouth was watering before they even made it to the table. Asad and Khayru both looked at Mahir and back at me. "Yes, boys, these are snacks. I will help you open them, and then you can eat them!" I couldn't keep my excitement to myself any longer. Mahir placed the snacks on the table. "Yes, mama is correct. These are granola bars, which have a delicious tasting and good for you." "And these are fruit snacks, which are sweet and are my favorite." Maimun comes over and takes a seat next to me. I lean into Maimun a bit and tease him. "I bet you only come here for the snacks, isn't that, right?" Maimun begins to blush, and I know I hit the nail on the head. My quiet, shy, second oldest could care less about making money. He was here for the treats, and that made her both happy and sad.

I waited until the children all had their fair share of snacks before taking anything for myself. I carefully unwrapped a chocolate chip granola bar, wanting to savor every single action involved with eating the bar. When the first bite hit my mouth, I felt a tear sneak out of my right eye. Before I could catch it, Asad, who had found his way back to my lap, reached his chubby little arm up and wiped the tear away. "It's 'kay mama, it's 'kay," his sweet, angelic voice, still learning how to sound each full word, made me begin to cry even more. I put my head down before anyone else could notice. I had to keep it together if I wanted a chance to speak with the nurse or a doctor in private. When I straightened back up, I noticed Malika staring at me from across the table. I know she is calculating everything in her head. She is replaying what happened at the bath, to the walk here, to all the interactions between her father and me, and now witnessed me eat this granola bar as if I had eaten one before and was thinking back to a different life; she wasn't wrong in any of it.

Once we were finished with our snacks, Mahir led us over to a line of other Iraqi villagers. He instructed us that we would need to wait in this line and when we got to the front, he would be there to meet with us again. Ah yes, he and Maimun needed to go to work; translating for the other medics. The children waited in line, Malika and Lulu being more patient, while the younger boys ran circles around me, giggling. I instructed them that as long as they stayed near me and did not get too loud, they could play. In a very odd way, I imagined this was how it could be if I had not been a prisoner. This must be what it was like for other mothers with their children in this land.

As we got closer to the front of the line, I saw a beautiful woman, more than likely of Hispanic descent, giving out the vaccinations. Mahir was her translator, and they laughed between conversations with the families they helped. I wondered once we got up there if Mahir would stay by her side or if I could get him to leave for a moment. I needed at least one minute alone with this woman to give her some sort of sign about me.

When we were the next family in line, Mahir smiled proudly at me, and even though he could not see my face, I smiled back. I knew he could tell I was smiling by the creases around my eyes. "Rosita, I would like for you to meet my mother." Mahir had one arm behind his back, and he extended his other arm and gave me a slight bow. I bowed back and nodded my head down; all my courage had drained from me. The way Mahir was standing there froze me in my tracks. He was the identical image to his father- my captor. I couldn't even remember my plan anymore. All I could see was Mohammad, the first time, he allowed me out of my hole and was showing me my new 'home' where I would finish my pregnancy.

I heard a woman's voice and realized Rosita was speaking to me or someone. I looked up, and both she and Mahir were staring at me. "It is so nice to finally meet you, Ma'am. Mahir has spoken so highly of you." Ma'am? I could not figure out why they were calling me that, and then it occurred to me that the children did not know my name. "Ah, yes, thank you." I stuttered out a few words so she would not think I was a complete idiot and put my head back down. Mahir finished introducing the children and began to write down all their names and ages on a notecard. He then handed that over to Rosita, who had already begun to work on the children. Malika went first to show the younger children that it would not hurt. Lulu went next, always wanting to be just like her big sister. The younger boys were both scared, so I took one of their hands in each of mine and walked up together. Rosita dropped the cotton ball she had just grabbed from her station when she made eye contact with me. I looked down once again, not sure what to make of it. She cleared her throat and grabbed another cotton ball.

"Wow, I can say that I have been here for several months, and this is the first time I have seen several children, all with such gorgeous green eyes, but I see where they get them from. Ma'am, your eyes are breathtaking." I was already struggling with words, but now, I truly had nothing to say. A new fear went through me when she said the next thing. "Okay, boys, your mama is a brave woman, so she is going to roll up her right sleeve so I can give her shots. Once you see her take them, you two will be next." I realize this could be my chance. My right arm had one identifier on me that surely would make this woman wonder who I was. I let go of the boy's hands and slowly roll up my right arm sleeve, turning my wrist to the right so she would not be able to miss looking at the scars and the faded remnants of what once was beautiful scrolling cursive letters. I stared at the woman as she leaned in to give me my shots, praying that she noticed my arm and it would trigger some sort of curiosity within her. If she had any suspicions, she had an amazing poker face because she finished with me and then moved on to Khayru and Asad. I hadn't even noticed that I had been holding my breath the entire time, and once she was done with the boys, I let out an exhale. "Now, that wasn't so bad, was it?" Rosita asked the boys as she rubbed the tops of each of their heads. They both giggled at her as she began to clean up the wrappers from the Spider-Man Band-Aids she had given to each of them. "Well, again, it was nice to meet you, Ma'am.

Please know that Mahir and Maimun are doing an exceptional job of helping us translate. I know that myself, and many of my other peers- like Tara, are grateful for their help."

At the name Tara, my heart skips a beat, and I make direct eye contact with Rosita, and she winks. Could she be talking about my Tara? Oh my God, could my sweet Tara be HERE? In Iraq? At this point, Mahir is directing us off to another tent, and I can't help but look back at Rosita. She is still sitting there, but she looks at me and holds her right arm up, and I know she saw it. I don't know what this will mean or if my Tara is here, but I nod and follow Mahir. At some point, I grab on to both the younger boys' hands, squeezing them tightly.

Chapter Twelve

TARA

After a week of being on the road, travelling from village to village, Tara was no closer to finding her mom than she had been when they left the medical village. She had tried not to let her disappointment show in front of Nick. He had been so supportive all week. Any time there was any female who seemed suspicious or acting too shy with the medics, Nick would alert Tara, but they were all dead ends. She didn't know just how many of these smaller villages were on the outskirts like this, but they definitely had not been to Mahir's village. At some point, she had to think they would have run into him or Maimun since they slept outside whatever village they had worked in all day. Tara was beyond exhausted and thought about not only her mom but her dad too. All the missions and deployments he had been on over his career. He barely talked about the details of his missions, but she knew he had seen some pretty serious stuff in Iraq and Afghanistan. She thought back to their last call a few weeks ago and remembered that even though she had told him she loved him, she had hung up, slightly disappointed in her father. He didn't want her to get her hopes up on searching for her mom, but she couldn't give up. Being out in the villages only made her think about her mom even more. Was she imprisoned somewhere deep below the ground where no one would ever find her? Saddam Hussein had been known for having underground bunkers and hiding spots. Could the insurgents have been keeping her alive underground all this time? Or was she dead? Her bones buried in a shallow grave somewhere? She shuddered, thinking about that last question. Even though she didn't want to think that, even she knew that was a strong possibility.

They rolled back into the medical village after hours. All families looking for vaccinations were gone for the day. All medics and equipment packed up until the next morning. Tara helped unload the jeep and grabbed her bags. Nick walked her back to her tent, sensing her disappointment in the uneventful week. "You want to drop your bags and see if there are any leftovers from dinner left?" Nick asked her as they walked up to the entrance of the female tent. Tara sighed and looked up at her fiancé, wondering how she had gotten so lucky to have him in her life. "You go ahead without me; I am beyond exhausted and just want to go to sleep." Nick gave her a quick kiss before turning around to head to his tent. Tara walked in and pulled back the fabric she had strung up as a curtain. She was startled to find Rosie sitting on her bed with the biggest shit-eating grin on her face.

"Chica, you are NOT going to believe what happened while you were gone." Rosie moved over so Tara could sit down next to her on the cot. Tara truly had no clue what could have happened that Rosie had to share the gossip about right now, but Tara was not having it. "Look, Rosie, I am so tired. I just can't stay up to talk about what or who did what while I was gone." Tara began to untie her hiking boots and kicked them off, the layers of encrusted sand making a mess on the mat she had underneath her cot. "Look, I know I am the queen of gossip and illegal hooch around here, but this is something that you need to hear right away. The day you guys left on your week-long adventure, Mahir brought the rest of his family back here to get their shots." Tara stopped taking off her socks and looked up at Rosie. She recalled that just the night before Tara and Nick had left, she had shared everything with Rosie, including her suspicions about Mahir's mom and family.

"And what happened? Did you get to see the rest of his family?" Tara was trying to be patient, but she needed to know everything like right now. "Chica, not only did I see them, but I was the one that helped them. And Chica, I have been waiting this entire week to talk to you. Doc's satellite phone wasn't working while you guys were gone. Trust me, I tried calling you every night you were gone. You were not only right about your gut instinct about your mom, but I am pretty certain Mahir's mom is your mom too." Rosie began to cry, and Tara joined her. How could this be? How could she be so confident in what she was telling Tara right now? These were dangerous feelings to have, optimistic feelings when Rosie had only been told the story of Tara's mom just one day before this encounter?

Tara turned, so she was completely facing Rosie, and grabbed Rosie's hands. "Rosita Montoya, you know how severe of a statement you are making right now. Please, tell me, what makes you think Mahir's mom is my mother?" Rosie took what was holding her hands and twisted Tara's right wrist around. "Because Chica, Mahir's mom had this same tattoo that you have. And if that was not enough, her eyes were like looking straight into your eyes. I'm telling you with everything inside of me, Mahir's mom is Emily Sanders."

Chapter Thirteen

JOSH

R etirement was not all that it was cracked up to be for a Special Forces soldier. Josh Sanders still found it difficult to sleep in later than 04:30, or as many soldiers called it, zero-dark thirty. Even in his early forties, Josh got up every day before the sun rose to get in at least a five-mile run and another hour of good old fashion PT. Sometimes, he would meet up with other retirees that had all settled around Ft. Bragg after retirement. One of his closest buddies was Rodriguez, who had not served with Josh but had served with Emily and been with her when she was ambushed. Even after all these years, Roddie, as Emily had called him, still felt he needed to stay close to the Sanders family. Even though Josh had remarried after the girls had grown up and moved out, Roddie and Josh still got together at least once a week to work out and catch up on each other's families.

This particular morning, Josh was alone with his thoughts. Dina, his second wife, was a civilian. She was supportive of his continued need to fill the gaps that the military had left behind. They had waited to marry until both Tara and Alicia were on their own, but he had been with Dina shortly after Emily had been declared dead. Josh had devoted eight years to finding Emily, and when the Army finally threw in the towel, Josh had been in a dark place. His commander at the time had ordered him to attend counseling. Dina was the receptionist at his therapist's office. He had no intent in falling in love with her, but visit after visit, Dina would check him in and make cheerful small talk with him while he waited in the lobby. Over time and many hearts to heart sessions with his therapist, he decided to take a chance and asked Dina out for coffee. From that point on, he found in Dina, an anchor he hadn't known he needed. She was nothing like Emily, and he loved her for that. As much as he had no intentions of ever forgetting the first love of his life, he needed to move on if he wanted to give his daughters any sort of normalcy to grow up with.

So here he was, lacing up his shoes and hitting the pavement. Dina knew he still loved Emily and knew this was his time to talk to her. When he came back after his two-hour workout sessions, she knew Josh Sanders was all hers, and she could accept that.

This run was special. Today would have been his and Emily's 20th wedding anniversary. His therapist always told him to feel his feelings. Don't just tuck them away into another compartment. So, he intended to run for however long it took to feel all his feelings this morning. He thought about the day he first saw Private First-Class Emily Moore, looking like a lost puppy reporting to her new duty station. He knew within seconds of making eye contact with her that he was going to marry her. He hit his buddy in the side and said, "You see that PFC? I'm going to ask her to marry me one day." His buddy snorted and laughed, "Roger that Sanders, Roger that." But Josh held true to his word.

Within six short months of knowing each other, Josh had convinced Emily to fall in love with him, and they were planning their marriage before being shipped off to Korea for a year. Their deployment to Korea would never happen because Emily found out she was pregnant soon after saying their vows. Both Josh and Emily were able to have their orders changed so that Tara could be born with her mom and her dad present. Everything about their marriage was perfect.

Emily was a strong, independent female soldier, and that was exactly what Josh needed since he was a sergeant in the Special Forces. He was constantly leaving on six-month deployments or trainings, and Emily never flinched or complained. She was rock steady, and she had a motto that he loved. Always Forward is something she would always say whenever he had doubts about upcoming trainings or deployment. She would tell him, "We only move in one direction- Always Forward. So, get out there and do what you need to do." He could still remember her deep green eyes and how she could make all the heads in a room turn with her smile.

Her looks weren't the only thing he thought about on his run, he thought about how dedicated she was not only to the Army but also to being a mother. She would pump in the field and have a runner bring her breast milk back to base when she was out on a field exercise. She was determined not to let her military career get in the way of being the best mom she could be to Tara. He could still hear Tara and Emily laughing their heads off in Tara's room. Emily had a special knack at getting Tara to go from being upset to laughing in seconds.

Josh kept moving forward, always forward, just like Emily had always told him. One foot in front of the other, and before he knew it, the tears came, and he let them fall freely. He needed to feel this; he needed to feel his first true love's absence. The black hole that had taken up so much of his heart was still there, no matter how much Dina loved him, and he needed to feel it all. He thought about what could have been if he had pushed her to request a delay in her deployment. For God's sake, Alicia was just a baby when she had left. If only he had tried harder, Emily would still be here, and their lives would have been different.

After a grueling three hours of running, Josh made his way back home. Unsure if it was the emotional or physical exhaustion, he collapsed on the steps of his front porch. He was slouched over when he heard a voice coming from the corner of the porch. "You look a little tired, Master Sergeant." Josh knew that voice without even looking up. He began to untie his running shoes when he replied, "I guess working out will do that to a man. You should try it sometime, Roddie." Josh turned around and stood up to greet his buddy properly. They fist bump, but then Roddie brought Josh in for a bear hug. "I figured you could use some company today." Roddie seemed to remember every detail about Josh and Emily's life, but Josh guessed that had more to do with the overwhelming guilt that Rodriguez had lived with since that hellacious day, so many years ago. "Thanks, man, I appreciate it, but I think I am good. I ran my literal ass off and worked through some shit on the pavement." Josh grabbed a water bottle he had purposely left on the porch before he had left that morning. Dina would already be gone for work, and she hated when he trekked through the house dripping in sweat after his workouts. Josh motioned to the front door, "You want to come inside, and I can fix us some breakfast?"

Rodriguez smiled and said, "Hell yes, brother! I will never turn down a free meal," as he slapped Josh on the back as they headed inside.

After breakfast, Rodriguez was helping Josh clean up the kitchen when he paused while loading the dishwasher. Josh noticed the break in the sound of plates hitting the rack. "Roddie, you do know the dishwasher isn't going to load itself, right?" Roddie lets out a long sigh and goes back to dish duty. "I didn't want to tell you this, especially not today, but I have been having those dreams again. The ones about Emily in the Humvee." Josh closed his eyes and stopped wiping the counter. Roddie had gone over these dreams with him so many times, to the point that Josh felt like they were his dreams too. "The one where you pull her out of the truck?" Roddie stops loading the dishwasher again. "Yeah. I pulled her out and saved her and Grant. Damn, why couldn't I be the fucking hero I was in my dreams? Why didn't I try harder, Josh?"

Josh turns around and stands nose to nose with Rodriguez. "You stop that shit right now. You hear me? You have lived with this guilt too fucking long, and it ends now." Josh felt terrible coming off so aggressive, but he knew this was the only way to get through to his best friend. Rodriguez looked away and wiped at his eyes, "I know, brother, but now Tara is over there, and all I can think about is what if something bad happens to her too?" Hearing Rodriguez say this is like a sucker punch right to Josh's gut. "Don't go there, Roddie. Don't fucking go there. Don't you think I think about that every day? Both my girls are gone and there is not a damn thing I can do to protect them."

Josh walks away from his best friend and takes a seat at one of the barstools at the kitchen counter. He takes a moment to calm himself down so he can collect his thoughts before he continues. "Look, Tara is smart, and she is safe. She's not leaving the wire, and where she is at is considered at peace. We have to trust that she is in good hands. Can we just leave it at that? Please?" Josh had already been down the same roads Roddie was going down when it came to Tara, and he had to tell himself she was safe; otherwise, he would drive himself mad.

Chapter Fourteen

TARA

~

Tara sat there, holding hands with Rosie, staring down at the tattoo she had on her right wrist. She had begged her dad to let her get it when she had turned 16. He didn't love the idea, and of course, Dina had opinions about it, but in the end, he went with her to get the tattoo. Even at 16, it meant more than just getting the same tattoo that she knew her mother had on her wrist. She was already plotting her future, and she knew at some point she would need to have the same identification tool like a tattoo to be able to find her mother. It hadn't hurt, just stung a bit. Her dad sat in a chair across from where she sat on the tattoo artist's bench with his head down. She knew this was difficult for him since he had been with her mom when she, too, had gotten the original tattoo. Tara could only imagine what was going through his mind at that time. She felt terrible making him go with her, but she needed a consenting parent to give the okay for the tattoo.

"Tara, Chica, you haven't said anything for like 30 minutes. Are you in there?" Rosie squeezed Tara's hands, and Tara looked up at her. "Oh, um, sorry. I guess I spaced out for a bit. I don't even know what to say or think right now. I have waited for this my entire life, and now I don't know what to do next. Do I tell Nick? Do I call my Dad? Tell Doc? Rosita, help me figure this out!" Tara was beginning to panic, breathing shallow breaths, on the verge of a panic attack.

Rosie sat back and closed her eyes. When she opened them back up, Tara could tell she had a plan from the look in her eyes. "Okay, Chica, this is what we are going to do.

First, you are going to talk to Nick about it. He's your number one and your rock. He deserves to know this before you take any action. Once you talk to him and share the rest of my plan with him, we go to Doc. I don't think we need to tell your Dad yet. Just think if I'm wrong? Chica, that would crush your Dad's soul. So yeah, we go to Doc, explain everything to him, and then we see how we can contact the military and our government to get her out of here." Tara took a deep breath and closed her eyes. She envisioned having to share everything again with Doc, and although she knew it was going to be difficult, she took another deep breath and opened her eyes. "Alright, let's go talk to Nick. This can't wait until morning."

Tara waited outside the male tent while Rosie snuck in to find Nick. The medical village had strict rules that men and women could not cohabitate and were not even to enter the other sexes' tents. Lucky for Tara, Rosie was not a rule follower. Since it was after lights out, Rosie snuck in and dragged Nick off his cot. Nick came shuffling out of the tent; clearly, he had fallen asleep as soon as his head hit his pillow. "Okay, ladies, this better be worth it. I had just started dreaming about eating an amazing Big Mac." Nick was rubbing his face, trying to wake up still.

Tara got straight to the point, recounting everything Rosie had shared with her, with Rosie chiming in when Tara got a few details wrong. "Holy shit Tara!" Nick yelled but in a whisper. "How are you not more excited right now? Your mom is alive, and she's not that far away! What are we waiting on? We got to go tell Doc!" Nick began pacing back and forth, which was normally Tara's style. Tara grabbed him to stop pacing; for some reason, the movement was making her motion sick, or maybe that was just her nerves and the adrenaline coursing through her veins at the moment. "Nick, this is all I have ever dreamed about, and I trust that Rosie saw what she saw, but I can't act irrationally. We need to think this through and be careful. If that is my mom, that means that she is still being kept captive. Yes, her captor allowed her to come here to get shots, but with her children. I have to consider the fact that Mahir and Maimun could be part of their father's plans. We do not approach Mahir or his brother tomorrow, and I do want to talk to Doc, but at this hour, I don't know if that is the wisest choice. I know this is a bombshell that was just dropped on us, but I think we need to sleep on it tonight." Tara couldn't even believe the words that came out of her mouth, but she knew she was right, and so did Nick and Rosie. They all nodded in agreement, and they all went in at the same time for a group hug. Tara was hit with a flood of emotions. "Thank you both so much for believing in me. I don't know what I would do without you both." Rosie rubbed her back and said, "Chica, I am so grateful you opened up to me when you had. Otherwise, we would not be standing here right now. I would have had no clue and helped the woman and her family and moved on with my day. Thank you for being brave and strong enough to never give up on your mom."

Tara and Rosie left Nick to try to get some sleep. They all agreed they would meet with Doc first thing in the morning before the workday began. When Tara made her way back to her cot, she was physically and emotionally exhausted, but there was no way she would be falling asleep any time soon. Tara reached for her faded picture of her mom that she kept under her pillow. It was so old and worn from Tara holding it so much but the woman staring back at her was still there and fully visible. If she strained her memory enough, she could hear her mom laughing. It was so contagious and always turned Tara's bad moods around when she was little. If Rosie was right, what would her mom be like now? Would she remember how to laugh and be happy? Or would the potential physical and mental trauma have been too much to deal with? Tara laid the photo on her chest and stared up at the ceiling of the tent. She tried to calm her breathing and her mind. She needed to get some sleep; she would be no use to her mom or anyone if she was beyond exhaustion.

The next morning, Tara, Rosie, and Nick made their way to Doc's office tent before the workday was set to begin. They knew Doc would be in there finishing up paperwork from the day before and preparing for the day ahead. The sun was barely beginning to rise over the mountains when they entered. Tara and the crew entered when Doc said to, and Tara immediately began to word vomit her entire story and their theory on Emily Sanders.

"So, you are telling me that you think your mom is Mahir's mom, and I need to call the US Army?" Doc was sitting back in his makeshift office chair, staring back at Tara, trying to process the Intel dump Tara had just unloaded on him. "Look, I know this sounds absurd, but like Rosie said, the woman has the SAME tattoo as me. I specifically got this tattoo to look just like my mother's. What are the odds that an Iraqi woman, who has no access to a tattoo parlor, was able to get the EXACT SAME tattoo as me?" Tara leaned forward, trying not to lose her patience on Doc. She knew going into this conversation would sound ridiculous. Doc sighed, "I just wished you would have been upfront about why you were really here. This could potentially bring unnecessary danger to everyone here and not to mention, bad press for the organization."

Tara took a deep breath and chose her words carefully. "Yes, I agree I could have been more forthcoming in my interview. However, I don't think you would have let me into the program then. For the record, I do believe in our mission and helping people here. I grew up learning about the varieties of cultures and lack of resources here from my dad. I truly want to help these people, but I also have an invested interest here because of my mom. Please, Doc, you have to make some calls. I don't want to call my dad until I have more solid proof that this is indeed Emily Sanders." Tara sat back and waited for Doc to respond.

Finally, Doc leaned forward and grabbed the satellite phone. "Okay, let me get moving on this before the day starts. I can't promise or guarantee we will have a resolution today, so for now, keep this between the four of us." Tara nodded at Doc and then looked back at Nick and Rosie, who had been standing behind her for support. They nodded back at her, and she couldn't help by smile. She was finally on a path to finding her mom. And come hell or high water, she was going to find and rescue Emily Sanders.

Chapter Fifteen

EMILY

~

The trek back to our village was a blur. I had told myself I would pay even more attention to all the details along the way, but all I could think about was that woman, Rosita, holding up her right arm to me. She knew. She knew who I was. But how? Could my Tara really be here in Iraq? The thought of my sweet little girl being in this country made me even more nauseous than the motion sickness from riding the donkey. Then I remember that she isn't a little girl any longer. God, she had to be in her twenties by now. I haven't had access to a real calendar since before I was captured, and the best I could do was guess the day and month by the seasons outside.

I have no idea what this will mean for me. All I can do is hope and pray that this Rosita knows what she is doing. I will go back to our village and our hut and act as though nothing has changed; that is all I can do now and pray that the monster stays away on more work trips. That would make getting through the days a little bit more bearable.

It was dark out by the time we got back to our village. The only lights on were those fortunate enough to have some sort of a generator to run one or two lightbulbs in their hut. We were not one of those fortunate huts. As we made our way up the last bit of dirt path to our hut, which was set the farthest back in the village, my heart sank at what I saw ahead. I could see his shadow standing in the doorway of our hut, looming like the monster he was, with his arms crossed over his chest. I could sense already that something was not right and took a deep breath, knowing I would be the one to pay whatever price there was to pay.

Mahir helped me off the donkey while Malika carried Khayru and Maimun carried Lulu. I had Asad wrapped in his swaddling around my chest, and the six of us walked up the path towards the monster. Malika and Maimun could sense something was not right and kept their heads down as they walked by him into the hut. I followed suit, doing just as they did, hoping if I did not make eye contact, he would allow me to lay down and get some rest. I walked inside and laid Asad down on his small bedding next to my makeshift bedding on the floor. As I stood back up, I felt a searing pain go through the base of my neck, and I collapsed to the floor. The strike came so quickly that I didn't even have time to scream.

I wavered on the edge of passing out but could still see blurry images and hear what I could only guess was other people yelling. I was on my stomach, and I rolled over onto my right side, which brought with it a whole new set of pain from old injuries. I forced my eyes to focus and realized it was Maimun and Malika yelling at their father in Arabic. He was screaming back at them, and then he did the one thing I had never seen him do before. His right arm came up and swung down across Malika's face. At this, I screamed and reached out, but I was paralyzed in place by the way he had struck my neck. He knew all too well where my weak spots were. My neck and spine had never quite healed right from the rollover after the blast. All it took was one strike to the nerves on the back of my neck, and I was immobilized indefinitely. I laid there, watching the horror unfold in front of me as if I was watching a real-life horror movie. Asad woke up and was now screaming alongside me. The younger children peaked in from the other room, but the twins, who had been left behind today, kept Lulu and Khayru at bay.

The blows kept coming on Malika as she crouched down on the floor, trying to protect her face and head. Maimun jumped on Mohammad's back and began pounding on him, but the monster had insurmountable strength. I knew this firsthand. When he was on a mission to bring pain and suffering to a person, there was no stopping him. After what seemed like an eternity of screaming and fists flying, Mahir appeared in the doorway. After we had arrived home, he had to take the donkey back to the elder who had lent it to us. Mahir stood in the doorway, holding his arms out to lean on the archway, surely in disbelief at what he was witnessing. After all the years of the children seeing the monster beat on me, they had never witnessed him hurting one of their own.

Mahir finally snapped out of the daze he was in and began to yell something I could not understand at Mohammad. Instead of coming from behind as Maimun had done, he walked directly into the line of fire between Mohammad's fist and Malika. For some reason, this registered with Mohammad, and he froze with his fist in mid-air. Of course, god forbid he strike his first-born son; his pride and joy. The only child he took any time with. His prodigy.

Mahir calmly kept eye contact with Mohammad and whispered something to him as Mahir grabbed the monster's fist and lowered it. Malika ran over to Maimun, who embraced her and began rubbing her back. I lay there, still, not wanting to even breathe for fear of what would happen next.

After a few moments in this frozen tension, Mohammad went into his pocket with his left hand and fished out the crystal the children had given me. My heart sank as I remembered how careless I had been with the monster being gone for several weeks. I had not been hiding it in a small crack in the hut. I had simply been tucking it into the folds of my bedding, and in haste to be cleaned up and then leave for the medical village, I had not even given the crystal another thought.

Mohammad looked over at me and threw the crystal directly at me, it ricocheting off my cheek. I heard a crack when the crystal made contact, and I could not be sure if this was from the crystal cracking or my cheekbone. He said something in Arabic in a bitter tone and spat on me as he walked out of the hut. Mahir looked at his father walking away, and I know he was torn as to whether he should follow him or stay here to clean up the mess his father had made. After a few seconds, Mahir looked back at his siblings in the doorway, who were all quietly weeping. He then looked over at Maimun and Malika, who were still sobbing uncontrollably. He finally landed on Asad and me, who had crawled over to me and was rubbing my arm. Mahir nodded with a solemn look on his face and walked out the doorway to follow his father. I closed my eyes and laid my head back on the dirt floor. I knew before he had even walked away what choice he would make. He was his father's prodigy, after all.

I woke up to several male voices, speaking in hushed tones. I was still lying on the floor where I had collapsed after being struck in the base of my skull. I immediately begin to panic; hearing these voices reminded me all too much of that day after the ambush. Me, sitting, leaning on the Humvee, trying my best to defend myself and whoever was left in convoy. I never did make it through our vehicle to see if Grant or any of the other guys were left behind. I only had gotten off several shots before the monster, and the others had captured me.

I remain still, hoping the hushed voices were not coming for me, even though I knew I would be mistaken. I reached my hand around to feel for Asad in the dark. He is gone, and I begin to panic. I can only hope that one of the older children took him to bed with them. The voices get closer, and I wish I was already dead because I feel like this might be it for the first time in a long time.

The men came in through the front doorway of the hut, and I felt their footsteps coming towards me. I stayed on my stomach, laying as flat as I could into the dirt. Someone crouches down and grabs me by the back of my hijab. I try to grab onto something, anything, but they are stronger than I am. I try to scream, but another man steps in front of me and shoves a rag down my throat. I begin to cough, but it's no use. They tie another rag around my head to keep the one in my mouth from being spit out. I keep my eyes open because I needed to see him. I need to know that this is his doing and show him after all this time; I am not afraid to die.

Chapter Sixteen

TARA

~

Doc instructed Tara, Nick, and Rosita to go back to work and not to share the information they had shared with him with anyone else. Tara was praying that she would not run into Mahir or Maimun. She knew of all people; she could not share anything or ask them anything. According to Doc, they did not have anything to do with her mom's initial capture, but they more than likely would be extremely loyal to their father. Tara and the others could not risk the boys knowing what was going on. Tara went through her day in a daze. She was helping patients, giving kids and mother's vaccine after vaccine, but she was not truly there. All she could think about was that Rosie had met her mom. Her mom was alive, and now they had to rely on the government to help her get her mom out of there. The same government that had declared her dead.

At the end of the work day, Tara was packing up her work station when she saw Doc walking towards her tent. "Hey, Tara," Doc leaned in under the awning of the tent, "once you are done here, meet me in my office." This wasn't a question but a demand, and she knew better not to ask any additional questions out here. Lucky for her, Mahir and Maimun had not shown up today. This both had made the day easier to get through but also gave her more anxiety. Were they instructed not to come back? Did they somehow know what was going on? She was letting her anxiety get to her, and paranoia was setting in. She nodded at Doc and finished packing up her area. She jogged back to the supply tent to turn in her bag and then made her way over to Doc's office tent.

When she entered Doc's office, Doc was sitting behind his desk, and there were two men she had never seen before standing along the far wall of the tent. Both men were dressed in tactical gear but not specific military uniforms. They also had full beards and leathered tan skin. They clearly had been in this area of the world for a while. Doc stood up and motioned for Tara to come in.

"Tara, I want you to meet SFC Matthews and 1LT Gomez. They are both Army Special Forces and know of your father." Tara's throat immediately dried up as she realized she hadn't called her dad yet. What if these guys had spoken to him? She didn't want her dad to know until they were fully certain that they had a solid and secure plan in place to get her mom out of there. Tara tried to swallow so she could speak, "It's nice to meet you both." She stuck her hand out, and in return, each one came forward and gave her a firm handshake just like her dad would have.

"Tara, it is an honor to meet you, and I think I speak for myself and SFC Matthews when I say, we are going to do everything we can to help you find your mom. I don't know your dad as well as SFC Matthews, but your father is a legend in our organization." 1LT Gomez looked back at Matthews and then back to Tara. She was at a loss for words. She didn't know these men personally, but because of their bond to her dad and the Army, they were dedicated to helping her find her mom. She kept back the tears; the last thing she needed was for these two Special Forces soldiers to see her cry. She nodded and took the only other seat in the tent while both Matthews and Gomez resumed their stance off to the side.

Doc sat back down and grabbed a manila folder off his desk, and opened it. "Tara, SFC Matthews, and 1LT Gomez both have been on an operation in this area for quite some time now. What they are about to explain to you, you have to understand that this cannot leave this tent. You cannot even disclose this information with Nick, Rosita, or even your family." The grave look on Doc's face sealed the deal that what he was saying was serious. "Of course, you have my complete word that what is said in here will be in confidence. Do you need me to sign a waiver or something?" Tara looked from Doc and then to the two Special Forces soldiers. SFC Matthews walked towards

Doc's desk to stand behind him. "Actually, yes, we do need you to sign a confidentiality agreement. You can take your time and read it, but it basically states that what information you may learn about the operatives in effect are completely confidential. You cannot disclose this information to anyone, not even a legal team if you ever chose to bring said people into the loop." Doc handed over a document to Tara, and she took what was offered to her. She skimmed over the document and truly could care less. She would do whatever these men needed her to do, as long as it meant they were getting her mom out of there. Tara signed the paper and handed it back to Doc.

"With that part done, let's get down to business Tara." SFC Matthews took a wide stance and crossed his arms over his chest. Even though technically 1LT Gomez was higher ranking than Matthews, Tara could tell that he was more of the seasoned soldier when it came to operations like the one they were going to plan. Tara leaned as far forward as she could in the chair before she fell out of it. She was prepared to do whatever they needed from her. "We have been observing several villages for the last few years. Yes, technically, all combat operations have ceased in Iraq, but I'm sure you understand how insurgents and rebel fighters work?" Tara nodded her head in agreement to SFC Matthews to show that she did understand. Besides having a father that was Special Forces, she had also studied every aspect of both wars. She could tell you complete details of every major operation that had been completed in both wars and could give you bios on every single Special Force, Delta, and Army Ranger ever killed in action. So yes, she understood the patterns and behaviors of insurgents.

SFC Matthews continues, "We have reasons to believe that there are local leaders of Al Qaeda that have been living in the surrounding villages for quite some time. They go about their day-to-day lives with jobs, families and fit right in. They are no longer trying to recruit new soldiers but maintaining what they do have." SFC Matthews pauses, and 1LT Gomez speaks up, "They essentially are buying time. Waiting for the right time to make their move." The two men nod at each other, and SFC Matthews continues. "Mohammad Baz has been a person of interest for some time now. With the information you provided to Doc here, we are now escalating our watch on his village and all his actions."

Tara tries to let that sink in, "Wait, so are you telling me that you are just going to 'watch' this man more? What about my mom? Rosita confirmed that she has the same tattoo as me. Why can't we just go in there and get her out?" Tara held her arm up to show the men the tattoo as if doing this would somehow convince them to drop all their military standard operating procedures for her.

"Look, Tara, we understand your sense of urgency to get your mom out of there, but we also have to think about the villagers and her children. They are all innocent bystanders, and the last thing we can afford is to have a combative situation on our hands. As we sit here talking to you now, we have boots on the ground near the village monitoring all activities. We know that she and the children made it back to their hut safely, and we have seen the children going in and out since they returned. Plus, Rosita's statement included that your mother appeared to be in decent shape when they came here for their shots. With that knowledge in hand, we have to continue with our plan and trust that she will be fine for a little longer."

Tara pushed herself back into the chair. This conversation had not gone the way she had hoped it would. She was prepared to go with them to the village and literally scoop her mom out of wherever she was living. But she knew these men were the experts, and she trusted them 100%. "Okay, I know you guys have this under control. What do you need from me in the meantime?"

The two Special Forces men looked back and forth and then to Doc. Clearly, they had briefed Doc ahead of time and were expecting him to be the bearer of whatever news was coming.

Doc folded his hands on the top of the desk and looked Tara directly in the eyes, "Tara, we need you to stay out of this moving forward. You will proceed to do the job you came here to do, and you will do your best not to interact with Mahir and Maimun. We plan on keeping them on payroll, but we do not want them to be alerted of anything suspicious that may make them go back and tell their father anything." Do nothing. That is what they wanted from her? Tara looked at Doc and then at each of the Special Forces men. She then looked down at her wrist; *Always Forward. H*er mom had lived by that motto and was still moving forward. Albeit she was a prisoner and had been a reproduction factory all these years, but she had not given up hope. She had continued to move forward, and Tara had to do the same, even if that meant that her role in this rescue mission was to continue to be a medic and do nothing to save her mother. This is how she moved forward; by doing nothing.

Tara left the Special Forces men and Doc behind in the office tent and wandered back to the female tent. She knew Rosita and Nick would want to know if Doc had looped her in on any developments. It was going to kill her not to tell them anything, but what would kill her even more was not being able to talk to her dad or her sister. God, she hadn't spoken to Alicia since she left for Iraq. Alicia was off doing her own thing down in the Caribbean, helping rebuild schools devastated by the previous year's tropical storms and hurricanes. All she wanted to do was tell them both that she had a lead, and it was a good one, but she could only imagine what that would do to her dad's psyche. How many times had he gotten a call in the middle of the night full of false hopes? She loved her dad too much to do that to him. So, she would avoid calling home for now since she couldn't trust herself not to slip and say something about her mom.

Chapter Seventeen

JOSH

J osh woke up at 3:00 am covered in a sheen of sweat. It was another replay dream, as his doctor liked to call it, where his subconscious went through all the events that surrounded learning about Emily's disappearance. His dreams were so damn vivid, from the male voice on the other end of the phone, one of Emily's officers explaining to him what had happened, to Josh, having to call Emily's parents and explaining it to them. He and his in-laws had agreed not to tell the girls right away. They were young, and he didn't think it would make things any better. Tara already asked about her mommy nearly every day, but baby Alicia couldn't complete full sentences yet. But in his dreams, it was like his brain had skipped past all the other details and always ended up him telling Tara that her mommy was lost. The look of confusion on her face was what always woke him up. To think that he had been through six combat tours, seen his amount of serious shit, but this was the dream that haunted him; his sweet Tara bug not understanding how her mommy could be lost.

Josh sat up and wiped his hands over his face, and grabbed the glass of water he kept next to the bed just for this reason. Dina began mumbling something as she lay on her stomach next to him. He rubbed her back, hoping she would remain asleep. He felt terrible for all the years of waking her up with his dreams. She was understanding to a point, but he knew that if it were up to her, all things of Emily would be erased from their lives. When the girls were in middle school, and Josh had explained to them that

Dina would be moving in, Dina had encouraged them to call her mom. Tara, being the oldest, defiantly drew a line in the sand and said absolutely not. Because Alicia followed everything Tara did, Alicia also continued to call her Dina.

As he looked back to the past, even though the girls obeyed Dina, they never truly loved her or even called her their step-mom. He knew this had hurt Dina, especially when Dina had tried to convince Josh that they should have one of their own. As much as Josh truly did love Dina, he couldn't bring himself to have any more children. In his own way, that was his line in the sand, and he was grateful to Dina for not pushing the issue.

He decided if he couldn't fall back to sleep, he might as well get up and get his run in early. He quietly got out of bed and grabbed his pile of running gear he always laid out on the floor the night before. Old habits die hard, and he would always plan out his days as if he was still an active Special Forces soldier. He disarmed the alarm on the house and crept out the front door. As he sat on the front steps lacing up his shoes, he thought if maybe he should tell his doctor the dreams were back, but he convinced himself to give it a few more days. It could just be that Emily was on his mind from their anniversary having just happened.

He stood up and did some quick stretches, and took off. He figured he could get in at least a solid thirteen miles and be back by the time he normally would get up. He could then head over to the gym and knock out a lifting session. He tried to focus on the present while he was running. He couldn't believe how much Emily had been on his mind lately as if somehow, she was sending him signals. He told himself it had to be due to the fact that both girls were off living their own lives, especially the fact that Tara was in Iraq. He hated her being there, and as much as he wanted to support her big dreams that her mom was alive, all he wanted was for her to let it go, but Tara had the same spirit and drive as Emily. Like he could never convince her to change her mind on a goal she had.

As he hit his stride, he confirmed that yes, that was why Emily was on his mind so much. It had now been several weeks since Tara had called last, and he knew she was safe since he still knew guys working over there. He really wanted to hear her voice and know she was indeed okay.

Josh ended up finishing up his half marathon and was more spent than he had planned. When he got back home, he had already decided to skip the gym. Maybe later in the day, he would get some sets in. That was the glory of being retired; he had all the time in the world now. He reentered the house, tiptoeing at first, but then he heard the shower, so he knew Dina was up. He went about his usual routine and got the coffee while he whipped up their protein shakes for breakfast. He stared at the blender, wishing he could do the same action to his brain to get rid of thinking about Emily. But it was more than just his thoughts; it was weird to think it, but it felt like on some molecular level, he could feel her. God, what if Tara was right? What if they had all given up on her, and she was still out there?

Chapter Eighteen

EMILY

―――――――――――――――― ❧ ――――――――――――――――

I knew before I opened my eyes where they had taken me. I could smell the earth around me. It wasn't just dirt and sand I smelled, but it was dried blood from my injuries that had bled down here all those years ago. It was the faint smell of urine and feces that lingered from having to use the bathroom in the far corner of the hole. I decide that I must already be dead, and this is hell. No human could ever be expected to go through this not once but twice. Then I hear the cover to the hole move back, and a small jug of water is lowered down on a string. I look up, trying to focus, but the sun is directly overhead, and I am temporarily blinded from being in the dark hole for who knows how long. Once my eyes focus, I see that it is not Mohammad but Mahir. The look on his face says it all. His father must have told him everything, and because Mahir worships the ground Mohammad walks on, he has joined forces with his father. There was no more love or devotion to Emily on Mahir's face. He looked like a soldier now, and this terrified her. This was always her suspicions that Mohammad had continually kept her pregnant to create his small army of insurgents. She took the water jug, and Mahir pulled the rope back up. She took a small sip of water, knowing all too well that this may be all the water she would get for a while. She laid back down and tried her best to remain calm. After all these years, she still had no clue where the hole they kept her in was. She knew it had been farther out from the village because she could never hear anyone until they were standing directly above the hole.

She closed her eyes and thought back to the beginning when she was down here. Her injuries had been so bad, she thought for sure she would need her right leg amputated. In the real world, she more than likely would have had it cut off. She replayed everything in her head- from leaving the girls and Josh behind to landing in Kuwait. She thought about the first convoy into Iraq and how they had felt like sitting ducks on MSR Sword in downtown Baghdad. Buildings and bridges everywhere, not knowing who was a friend and who was a foe. She thought about her guys, Roddie, Simmons, and Grant. They were her little brothers, always goofing off and playing pranks on each other. Even though they talked a lot of shit, she loved them, and they loved her. As the senior ranking NCO in their Humvee, they always did what they were told, even if they did grumble about it.

So many details were a blur now, but she could still remember the day they left on their last mission. Performing their preventative maintenance checks and services on their Humvee, or as they called it- PMCS, she had been bickering with Rodriguez about something stupid, probably, what type of cereal, Frosted Flakes or Fruit Loops was better. He always had a way of bringing up the dumbest topics to pass their time on missions. Others always thought they were genuinely fighting, but it was all in good fun. If she strained her memory, she could hear his deep, bellowing laugh.

Emily laid there and forced herself to remember everything she could. It brought on a painful headache, but she had to push through it. She opened her eyes and adjusted to the darkness again. She held up her right arm where the faded tattoo was located. She couldn't see it in the dark, but she knew it was there. *Always Forward*- that had always been her motto, mantra, whatever you want to call it. She couldn't just lay here and die. She couldn't let these monsters end her life. She needed to rest because the next time that cover opened up, she was going to fight her way out because there was only one way to go, and that was always forward.

Made in the USA
Monee, IL
17 September 2021

78293774R00050